Redford Branch Library
21200 Grand River
Detroit, MI 48219
313-481-1820

MICHAEL CORNELL

cara mia

STELLAR NOVELLAS

SEP 2021

Cara Mia
Copyright 2016 by Michael Cornell

Published by Stellar Novellas
10 Amherst Drive
Dearborn, MI 48120

Library of Congress Control Number:
ISBN: 978-0-692-74089-7

Cover Art: Francis Michael Dattilo, Jr.

Book Design: Words Plus Design

cara mia

Friday,
April 5, 1968

*Nation mourns assassination
of Martin Luther King, Jr.*

ONE

"Martin Luther's dead."

Martin Luther's *been* dead for centuries, Kinchen thought. He wasn't thinking.

"Mr. King," the old black man said, closing the elevator door. "They shot him."

"They?" Kinchen queried in abject belief.

"Sure. Didn't you see it on television?"

MICHAEL CORNELL

He hadn't been watching. He had worked late, rose early, hadn't even seen a newspaper.

"What's going on in the world, Mr. Kinchen?" old Evers wondered out loud. "First they kill Kennedy, last year we had the riots, now they kill Mr. King."

For some reason, the elevator walls seemed closer together, it occurred to Kinchen. He was standing against one wall while Evers manned the lever at the other, yet it seemed he could reach out and touch him without leaning.

The car jerked to a halt. The old man pulled back the accordion gate. Kinchen stepped out on Five.

"I don't know what's going on, Will," he said, stopping, then proceeded down the corridor to 506. By the time he had inserted the key, pushed the door open, he still hadn't heard the elevator gate close.

The office looked the same as it did six hours before. The cleaning woman had left it before he did. Kinchen headed for the tall front window, threw it open.

CARA MIA

"They shot him." The old man's words came back to him as he looked down on Grand Circus Park. They. The ones who shot JFK. The ones behind the riots. Will Evers was convinced *they* were behind it all. Kinchen was too tired, too confused to be convinced of anything and it bothered him. The days, the deadlines had begun to run together. When all jobs were urgent, then no jobs were urgent, was what he used to say when he worked for the big agency. Now the pattern was recurring at his and Deighton's own small ad shop. No wonder he couldn't give old Evers a cogent answer.

The telephone snapped the train of his thoughts. It was Deighton. He would be late, looking at couple of new suburban locations and no, he hadn't given the notion of staying downtown any more consideration than it warranted. Downtown was dead. We can argue it again at lunch, he laughed. More importantly, do you have the same craving for Mexican food that I have, he wanted to know.

Kinchen set the receiver down. Nothing about King, Martin Luther, not a mention. He stared out

MICHAEL CORNELL

at the park. An old woman in an olive-drab khaki jacket was feeding the pigeons. They looked much better fed than she did. A pretty blonde in a micro mini was strolling across the park on her way to work. Ten years ago, hell five years ago, that outfit would have gotten her arrested for indecent exposure. Now it just arrested admiring males. All except the young derelict lying on his back on a nearby slope. He looked to be around Kinchen's age from his fifth-floor lookout post, around twenty-eight, no older than thirty. The guy's left arm covered his face. His right arm was missing. Maybe he lost it in Vietnam in the tall grass.

There was a knock on the door. Come in, Kinchen called out. Doctor Stern entered, walked through the anteroom into his studio.

"Tragic about King," he shook his gray head. "They should hang the bastard who did it, right in the public square."

"Did you talk to Will?" Kinchen didn't know why he asked.

CARA MIA

"I didn't have to. He's taking it pretty hard. We all should."

The opening was sincere, but there was something else on Doctor Stern's mind. Kinchen could tell.

"Deighton and you are leaving, aren't you?" Stern finally asked.

The day was just beginning and once more Kinchen was slow with an answer. The question had been direct enough. So had old Evers' earlier.

"That's up to Deighton," he managed.

"Then you're leaving," the doctor concluded. "He told me he's been looking in the northern suburbs. "

"Listen, if it was up to me—"

"Then why don't you?" Stern didn't wait for him to finish. He had a way of doing that, making the point without mentioning it. If the equation was A, B, and C, he would invariably omit B. Kinchen was used to it after two and a half years. "You two *are* equal partners, aren't you?" was what Stern was asking this time without saying it.

MICHAEL CORNELL

"I let Adam worry about those things," Kinchen said evasively.

"Then do you mind if I worry about it, too?" Stern followed up wryly. "You two move out, then somebody else. Florida's too hot year round, Kinchen." The doctor was doing it again. By now, he should have been amused.

"How long have you been a tenant in the Fine Arts Building, Doc?" he wanted to know.

"The Fine Arts Building was in a different city then, Kinchen," Stern stated flat-out. "And contrary to what old Will thinks, the erosion set in long before last year's riots. When they shot Kennedy—"

"Why did you say that?" Kinchen broke in. "Why did you say *they* shot Kennedy?"

"Well, you didn't think it was only that little psycho in the book depository, did you?" Kinchen could not remember seeing the doctor so impassioned. "He only squeezed the trigger for them—nobody will ever convince me otherwise—but that gunshot sounded the death knell for our innocence as a country."

CARA MIA

"It may surprise you, Doc, but Will sets the date the same day you do," he said.

Stern did seem surprised, but only mildly. In what would have to qualify as the non-sequitur of the week, he said: "If you two leave, Kinchen, give me a few months' notice before you tell the landlord, okay? Right now, I've got a patient expiring in my office."

He watched Stern leave, knowing full well he never took any patients before nine o'clock. It was only eight-twenty, but he couldn't blame him for leaving. The doctor always had better answers for his own questions than he could provide.

It was just as well, Kinchen thought. He had his own patient expiring on the drawing board from the night before. It was called Fyfe Shoes' Spring-sational Sale and the fact that the words had been dubbed by the client afforded little consolation. He had already attempted to salvage the unsalvageable with a working subhead that read "Buy one shoe, get one free" but Fyfe's marketing director had left her sense of humor back at the university years before. Kinchen had once more come close to volunteering to return to Ann Arbor with her to look for it, but he figured it would cost him at least one year more than he could give it. Besides, that was Deighton's job. When he wasn't looking for a new office site, that is.

Kinchen hit the board, rendered a bulbous Mickey Mouse shoe, started staring out the window again. The one-arm guy had left. The old woman in the Army jacket was still there, but the pigeons had deserted her. Kinchen wanted to be with them, wherever they had gone. Instead, he spent the morning in place, behind the board, laying stroke after stroke of water color marker upon the layout pad, from Cool Gray to Warm Grey and back again. The pigeons returned, the old woman left and Adam Deighton arrived in time to go to lunch. They rode over to Mexican Villa in his Mustang.

At the villa, Deighton announced to him: "Business is moving to Southfield." He expected his partner to follow that declaration with another that he had located the ideal site for their next office. In-

CARA MIA

stead he said: "It's funny that they call it Southfield when it's a northern suburb."

Like Stern earlier, there was something else on Deighton's mind. He didn't have to ask what it was. "*This* is what you need, my friend," his partner intimated, leaning across the table. "If I weren't a married man, it is precisely what *I* would need."

Kinchen did not have the remotest of inklings what Deighton was referring to until he looked up from the menu and saw their waitress approaching. What he saw could not be waiting tables. The black hair, the dark eyes, the lithe figure said she was portraying Carmen in an opulent New York production. Only the order pad said otherwise.

"You are absolutely stunning," gushed Deighton, in his best straight-forward style. Generally, he left understatement to the subtlety of others. This time he had barely brushed the truth.

"That is kind of you to say," she replied undaunted. This was a woman who had long been accustomed to such praise, probably since age twelve, ten years easily.

MICHAEL CORNELL

"I'm not being kind, I'm being honest," Deighton advanced, as though taken aback by such nonchalance in the face of his blatant pronouncement.

Carmen effected the most cryptic of smiles without trying. "Honesty is always better than kindness," she said. The English was near perfect, with the faintest of accents; the response *was* perfect.

Kinchen looked away. He wanted to be headed where he was looking: the front door. The girl did not take his breath away. She made off with his brain. He hadn't felt a thing.

"May I take your order?" Carmen was asking him now.

He pointed at something on the menu without looking at her. Bare shoulders, the tightest of black pants left their table.

"Why did we come here?" he demanded of his partner.

"But I told you, old chum," Deighton grinned stupidly. "I just had a terrible craving for Mexican cuisine."

CARA MIA

"How many times have you seen her?" Kinchen wanted to know.

"Once. Last Saturday, but I was with Caroline and my dear wife always likes to sit in corners." Deighton dipped a corn chip into the salsa sauce. "Cara obviously is meant more for the open arena, wouldn't you say?"

"Cara?" It was close enough to Carmen, he thought.

"Ask me how I know?" his partner urged him.

Kinchen wasn't in the mood for tabletop games of any variety.

Deighton leaned forward again, said in a stage whisper: "I read name tags."

Monday,
April 8, 1968

*Racial unrest has erupted
in Chicago, Washington and
other major cities*

TWO

There was the slightest hint of perfume in the hallway and the door of their offices was open. Kinchen entered. The scent had preceded him inside and there were voices from Deighton's office. His partner had arrived before he had, on a Monday morning at eight-thirty. The perfume smelled fine, even alluring for this early in the day, but something else was amiss.

She was sitting in the chair in front of Deighton's desk and she did not look like a waitress anymore in the maroon silk suit with her nylon legs crossed demurely before her. She looked like someone interviewing for a job, except that she did not seem to be the least bit nervous about it. That seemed to be his partner's department.

"Well, what about it?" Deighton gave him the too-white smile. "The office could use some new inspiration, don't you think?"

Kinchen did not know what to think so he said nothing.

"Don't worry, old pal," laughed Deighton, getting up and coming around to the front of the desk, "Cara types, not terribly fast but accurately. I tested her. And her people skills are impeccable. Or is it unimpeachable?"

"I don't know, is it?" Kinchen finally said. He felt his partner's arm wrap around his shoulder.

CARA MIA

"We should talk," Deighton suggested, motioning toward the adjoining office, his studio. 'We'll be right back, my dear."

Kinchen could feel his friend's edginess through the tweed jacket. It disturbed him. The whole thing did.

Deighton shut the door, but *he* opened: "We're a small shop—'lean and mean' was the term you used—and we do not need a typist."

"But we could use somebody to answer the telephone," his partner responded defensively, lighting a cigarette as he did. "Hey, we both pay the bills around here, so don't think I'm retracting that 'lean and mean' business."

"Then what are you doing, Adam?" Kinchen inquired somberly.

"We're a small shop now, you're right about that," Deighton winged his way gracelessly, "but when we make the move to the suburbs, it's got to be more than you and me. It's one thing to have clients call and get no answer now—they think we're out there busting our humps for them—but when we've got new digs and look like a real advertising agency, we sure as hell better act like a real agency."

"*When* we make the move," Kinchen held his ground.

Deighton put his head down like a method actor getting into character. The hand with the cigarette was shaking slightly. "Listen," he began again in a quieter, softer tone, "why don't we give the girl a shot for a month. She can answer the phones, do a little typing for us, even some modelling for your ads and, who knows, maybe some client contact with me. For two hundred a week, she won't be a liability. If she is, we just say we're sorry."

"It's a lot easier to say we're sorry now," Kinchen remarked.

"But not a lot smarter. Cara will pay her way, I'm certain of it."

Kinchen felt himself going soft. The irksome part about it was that suddenly there seemed to be no guilt attached.

"One month,' he heard himself succumbing out loud, "then we take stock." He felt the arm on his shoulder again and, just as abruptly, the guilt had returned.

For the rest of the morning, the flow from the markers was slow, plodding. Hearing Cara answer the phone from the previously unused reception desk, and watching Deighton attempt to explain their pot-luck filing system to her, made concentration difficult. The sheen of her long black hair, the way she moved when merely picking up the receiver, and her low, smooth voice all seemed to compete with the layout pad before him. Noon, and lunch, could not arrive soon enough for him and, when Deighton asked if he would care to make it a threesome at the Chop House on Cara's first day, he declined without a moment's hesitation. Maybe now, he thought, the markers would work again.

Two minutes after they had left, Kinchen became acutely aware of how little the markers had to do with the completion of the layout at hand. As at the Villa, his brain had been pilfered and, with it, the creativity and skill to render even the most insignificant of advertising roughs. Against such formidable odds, he rose from behind the board, slipped his tweed jacket back on and left for lunch himself.

As he wandered in the general direction of Hudson's, the huge department store and indisputable hub of the downtown district, he tried to analyze the nature of the enigma. Cara Linda Cansino was a beautiful young woman. In his business, he had encountered hundreds of beautiful models and actresses. Cara was no more sophisticated than most, even less than some. And yet, none had possessed the initial presence to him. Of course, presence was generally illusionary, he reasoned. Familiarity killed it quickly enough. It was a real shame how quickly charisma eroded in the stark light of familiarity.

Kinchen looked up the entire vertical length of Hudson's eighteen stories and laughed to himself. Her name was Cara, not Carmen. Last week she had been waiting tables at Mexican Villa. This week she was trying out as receptionist with limited typing skills at their ad agency. Somehow he had allowed the frustrated fine artist within him to create this

CARA MIA

imaginary portrait in oils of a Latin temptress worthy of the palettes of the Renaissance masters. When he returned from lunch, he resolved, he would Cara Cansino in conversation, explain the work of an advertising art director to her, find out a little about her own background and destroy the whole insane illusion for good.

The light changed and Kinchen stepped with renewed energy toward the big store with the rest of the lunchtime throng. Inside, he took his time munching a hot dog at the fourth floor snack bar, then caught an elevator to the tenth floor record department. There, he perused the albums until he found himself studying the garishly designed *Sgt. Pepper's* cover of the Beatles for what must have been the fifty-second time. Despite the critical and commercial acclaim of the LP, he had resisted buying it on the grounds that the Fab Four had gotten too cute, too contrived with their music. Perhaps it was the transcendental influence of the yogi, it did not matter to him; all he knew was that the group had strayed from their roots: simple but more melodic three-chord progressions. Rock and roll would never be the same.

"Don't tell me you're the last person on earth who hasn't bought that record."

He looked up to see the pretty assistant marketing director of Herner's Ginger Ale, one of their agency's clients. With California-blond hair and soft-blue eyes, she contrasted sharply with Cara Cansino. The only parallel was the athletically slim shape and the stylishly short skirt of her suit. Now if he could only remember her name, the file would be complete. To his relief, she supplied it:

"Beverly Morehouse, Herner's Ginger Ale, don't you remember? I met you at the last presentation."

Kinchen was convincing in his mock indignity. "Please, give me credit for a longer memory than that," he said," even if you don't think much of my musical taste." He slipped the album behind two copies of *Rubber Soul*.

"Kitren, right?"

CARA MIA

"Kinchen, David," he smiled. "I guess we're even."

Her smile was pure California, too. "I loved the 'Bottled Magic' ad you did for us," she atoned.

"That's good," he decided to use the occasion for a little pre-sell, "because next week I'm bringing you guys a storyboard for a tv spot of the same concept."

"You mean I'll have to wait until next week to see you?"

Times really *had* changed. He wasn't about to complain about it.

"Is that an overture?" he feigned timidity.

"No, you fool, I'm asking you out to dinner," she volleyed, "unless, of course, you don't think it's such a good idea to mix in a little pleasure before business."

"Art directors are always looking for good ideas," he accepted.

"I'll call you."

Kinchen watched her walk off. The mini-skirt wasn't short enough, he determined. Those legs belonged on some Malibu beach with the rest of Beverly Morehouse.

He should have been buoyed. By two-fifteen, back at the office, he had all but forgotten Deighton and Cara had not returned from lunch. The guilt came rushing back. The concentration on his work never returned. He had been taken in by his own softness, his own clay-like pliability, Kinchen derided himself. He had let Deighton present him with a bill of goods and, like a fool, he had bought it all with the gullibility of a coupon clipper. At two-thirty, he put his jacket back on, started to leave.

They met him at the door. Deighton with that silly salesman's grin, Cara with that enigmatic smile. She was sober. With his partner it was hard to tell.

"Kinchen, old pal," Deighton beamed, making it even harder, "aren't you even going to stay to hear our good news?"

He didn't ask.

"Remember that great pitch we did for the convention business—the one that got away?"

CARA MIA

Deighton was sounding intelligible enough now. "Well, Cara and I ran into Summershoe at the Chopper and we got to talking. He tells me he's not all that enamored of the stuff he's getting from the Rogers Group and he'd like to review our material again. What do you have to say about that?"

It sounded promising, but he had nothing to say about it.

"Looks like Cara's paying dividends already," his partner steamed on. "Summershoe really took to her. He even wants her there when we re-pitch."

Cara had returned to her place behind the reception desk. Kinchen wanted to congratulate her, but he didn't know how. It was like congratulating someone for being beautiful.

Tuesday,
April 9, 1968

*U.S. rejects North Vietnam's
offer to negotiate peace*

THREE

There was nothing clever or mysterious about Cara's background. She had been born in a small village outside of Mexico City where she lived until the age of four when her family moved to Detroit. Her father worked in the Ford steel foundry and her mother waited tables part-time at the Villa while she and her younger brother attended public school.

MICHAEL CORNELL

Less than a year after she graduated from high school, her father disappeared. Six months after that, she returned with her mother to Mexico while her brother stayed on with an aunt in order to finish high school. Instead, he spent the better part of his seventeenth year in the Detroit House of Correction for various offenses, of which aggravated assault was the most grievous and attempted car theft was the pettiest. (Cara's candor in discussing the latter amazed Kinchen.) News of her brother's troubles *and* a growing disdain for the seeming purposelessness of the life in her tiny native village motivated her return. A nearly as meaningless string of odd jobs began and ended with stints in her mother's old work classification at the Villa where, of course, she had met Adam Deighton. Kinchen did not need to hear the rest. In fact, it had taken him a good day and a half to hear the first part when his partner finally broke away from the office—and Cara—to call on an impatient client.

With Deighton gone and Cara's story told, the markers began to flow once more. The last of the

CARA MIA

Fyfe shoe-sale roughs were finished and he showed Cara how to mount them on matboards so he could put the finishing touches on the Herner Ginger Ale television storyboards. She completed her task sooner than he expected and, with his approval, watched with keen interest and savvy inquiry as he finalized the *Bottled Magic* tv frames. Her scrutiny of his work was not the least bit intrusive to him. Conversely, the nearness of her, the light scent of fragrance she wore, served to inspire him in a way that was unfamiliar rather than unsettling. He even found himself fighting the inclination to delve into her personal life, where she lived, who she saw socially. The answer to the first question should have been on her employment application but Deighton had dispensed with such "formalities" in her case; the answer to the second question, Kinchen decided reluctantly, was none of his business.

Deighton returned in the late afternoon from what he described as a grueling session with the disgruntled client, the self-made founder of a fast-growing furniture chain. The man wanted a detailed breakdown of the agency's media recommendations for the placement of his radio and tv advertising through August and, typically, he wanted it by first thing tomorrow. To meet his demands, it would mean pouring through the Arbitron broadcast-ratings journals, assimilating the myriad numbers and weighing them against a host of other variables (from demographic age to income) to arrive at what should pass for an intelligent and commercially viable media plan. It would also mean holding Cara over to type the proposal and to assist in the compilation of the figures. Except for the last part, Kinchen was relieved to be a Creative Director, a writer-artist type with little patience and less aptitude for such necessary evils. As such, he would not be expected to stay over to suffer through the proposal's preparation.

Beverly Morehouse called around five-fifteen and Kinchen immediately accepted her invitation for dinner at her apartment that evening. In doing so, he felt little compunction over leaving his partner. As so often had been the case of late, he had

CARA MIA

worked straight through lunch, with only a bag of chips and a Coke providing transient energy sans sustenance. Besides, he thought, Cara's company afforded attractive compensation for Deighton's overtime labors.

The Rivard, once the proverbial last word in urban elegance, still furnished an impressive downtown address for young professionals whose stars were ascendant on the local business scene. Beverly Morehouse's comet was not only ascending, if comets performed such maneuvers, it was soaring. Three times over the last eight months her picture had appeared in the Free Press' *On the Move* column. The picture, of course, may have had something to do with that, Kinchen was convinced. It looked more like a publicity glossy for a young movie actress than the assistant marketing director of a soft drink company. Or did the last newspaper blurb refer to Beverly as an *Associate* marketing director? He couldn't remember as he padded his way on the plush carpet toward her apartment on the Rivard's top floor.

MICHAEL CORNELL

"Did you bring the 'Bottled Magic' storyboards with you?" was the first thing she said upon opening the door, but the faintest hint of a smile told him at once that business was not the order of the hour.

"I gave them to the doorman downstairs for last-second modifications," he said, entering the apartment. The eclectic collection of antique furnishings and bric-a-brac spoke of old Grosse Pointe money, not the salary of an up-and-coming marketing whiz. The head man, her boss, couldn't have been doing *this* well. He tried to ignore the aura of pretense, but it wouldn't be easy; even the smell of the surroundings had a reverential air about it, more cathedral than museum.

"Mother is an interior decorator," she said with an apologetic tone that made him feel like an amateur actor, easy to read and easier to impress. It made him angry at himself, because he was *not* impressed, he was sure of it.

"I didn't say anything," he remarked as matter-of-factly as he could.

CARA MIA

"You didn't have to," she returned, leading the way into the dining room. Suddenly, he found himself wishing he was not following her. The shortness of her orange terrycloth outfit, somewhere between the regulation length for a tennis player and a figure skater, made that seem improbable.

Dinner by the natural glow of the twilight sky was excellent. Medium-rare filet mignon topped with a French sauce he had never heard of and couldn't pronounce if he had. It reminded him of something Orson Welles had said on the Dick Cavett talk show about the French burying perfectly good food under their smothering sauces. Except Beverly Morehouse's dinner had been superb on all counts.

Conversation, too, had been pleasant, with small talk about work and career directions providing the fare. It was while they sat on the antique oriental carpet sipping white Rhine that the course shifted to a more personal nature but, even then, work furnished the springboard.

MICHAEL CORNELL

"I'm thinking about New York," she informed him in the sort of tone normally reserved for announcements to long-established acquaintances. It was as though she were already fishing for a reaction, his reaction. "If you're any good at all, you're going to end up there anyway. If you're not, you might as well find out as soon as you can."

When a response did not seem forthcoming, she rose and went over to the stereo, put a record on. He had followed her over with his eyes, her graceful glide and long legs diverting his attention from the now deep-blue velvet of the night sky. When she returned to sit down beside him, *that* record was playing. Sgt. Pepper did not sound any better to him tonight, even with the wine. She seemed to sense it, but said nothing. Instead, she leaned close, kissed him with a gentle familiarity that should have surprised him but didn't.

"Why did you tell me about New York?" he asked as their lips separated.

"It was silly, wasn't it?"

"Was it?"

CARA MIA

"You hardly know me and already I'm telling you that I may be leaving soon." The words *did* have an absurdity about them, yet there was a rationality to them that defied logic. "Why *did* I tell you about New York?"

"Because you wanted me to be the first one to know," was his reply.

"How did you know I hadn't told anyone else?"

"The wine told me," he smiled, leaned forward, kissed her. When his hand dropped to her bare thigh, she simply removed it, but continued to kiss him.

"Sorry," he said after.

"For what?" she asked as though completely oblivious to his advance.

"I forget," he answered, the confusion setting in again. Maybe it was that awful record.

"That's just it, you *will* forget when I go to New York. You'll fall madly in love with *her* and this night will be just another page on a desk calendar."

"Her?"

MICHAEL CORNELL

"Your new assistant. I talked to Adam on the phone this morning and he told me about her. He says she's quite exotic looking."

It was so funny, he thought. He had actually forgotten about her, being with Beverly at dinner, sipping wine, lying on the floor here in the darkness of her quiet cathedral. It was as though Cara had walked in through the locked doors, up the aisle, stood before them.

When he left the Rivard at sometime after eleven, he tried to fight the impulse to drive by the Fine Arts Building. He could not. The light was still on in their fifth-floor office.

It did not seem funny to him at all, not the night, not anything about it.

Wednesday,
April 10, 1968

*South Vietnamese President Nguyen
requests full-scale mobilization*

FOUR

Kinchen did not feel like talking. The minute after he stepped into the office early the next morning, Doctor Stern stepped in behind him. It was difficult not to engage the man once he got going and he was going again on the same routine.

MICHAEL CORNELL

"So when you leaving?" Stern asked, wandering behind Kinchen's vacant drawing board.

"Nothing to report," he said, wondering where the woman at the donut shop had hidden the cream for his coffee. "When something comes off the wire, you'll be the first to know, Doc." He corrected himself: "No, you'll be the second to know. Deighton will be the first, you'll be next, I'll be third. I'll get it from you."

The doctor smiled his lopsided smile, began filtering through rough layouts on his credenza. "You should see *my* drawings," he laughed. He didn't say I wish I could draw like you; he said you should see how I draw. Next, he would mention his brother-in-law.

"I know: your brother-in-law is a creative genius." Kinchen beat him to it.

"You know Stu?"

"I know *of* him."

"Stu Frankel, the one-man ad machine, I call him," he piped up. "Except he should take on a partner. He just turned fifty. How much time can an ad man have after that?"

"Depends on how seriously he takes the business," ventured Kinchen.

"Or how seriously he takes himself," Stern came back. "Would you like to meet Stu?"

"For what purpose?"

"I just told you: he just turned fifty. When he's in the parlor, he won't need a partner anymore." The doctor started on his way out. "What about it?"

"What about *my* partner Deighton?"

"Let him move to the suburbs," Stern added as he was nearly out the door: "Just make sure he leaves *her* behind."

Kinchen watched the door close, heard it click shut. He wanted it to open again, to watch her walk through at that very moment, to ask her how long she had stayed with Deighton the night before and what they had done together.

He had finished his coffee and the black, non-sugared one he had bought for his partner when the door click finally disturbed his ritualistic survey of

MICHAEL CORNELL

Grand Circus Park. It was twelve after nine when she walked into his studio with the blue binder under her arm.

"It's a copy of the first half of the proposal Mister Deighton and I worked on last night," she announced as she placed the binder down in front of him.

He pretended to look at it with some interest. He was looking at the sleek black-and-white dress that curved gracefully to a juncture eight inches above her knees.

"What happened to the second half?" he continued the play-acting.

"Mister Deighton has the original of the first and second half for his meeting with the client; the copy machine broke down shortly before I left last night. That's why I had to stop and make a copy of the proposal portion for you this morning from last night's first draft. Mister Deighton had said you wouldn't be interested in the numbers half."

Neither portion interested him. Surely she could tell. He asked: "What time did you two leave?" although he had distinctly heard her use the pronoun "I".

Cara did not answer right away. When she did, it was open-faced, direct: "I left around ten-thirty. I do not know how late Mister Deighton stayed." Kinchen thought he detected the smallest measure of resentment in her voice, as though he had insulted her. He had, and his partner as well.

"What time was Adam's meeting?"

"He only said it was for breakfast; he did not specify an exact time," she answered as he groped for something else to ask her. It was too early to look ravishing, he thought, but the set of her features and the subtlety of her makeup, her eye shadow, said otherwise.

The telephone disrupted his reverie. Cara leaned forward to pick it up, but his nervous energy had somehow placed the receiver in his hand before her. When the client from Fyfe Shoes spoke, he felt foolish. As with Beverly Morehouse the evening before, he was giving everyday dramatics a bad name.

MICHAEL CORNELL

The client urgently requested a small change in the art for next day's newspaper insertion. Kinchen assured the man he would take care of it himself and even drop it off at both papers before the afternoon deadlines. The client thanked him, calmed down enough to make a joke about the business they were in. Kinchen pretended it was amusing, hung up.

"What are you doing for lunch?" he stabbed.

"I have to go to Hudson's to get something to send to my mother for her birthday." Again her tone was straightforward but it sent the rollercoaster hurtling south, just as her revelation about leaving the office at ten-thirty the preceding night had propelled it due-north. Kinchen was not the bumbling actor anymore; he was the bumbling schoolboy. The spin on the coaster, he thought, was becoming rife with tragicomic possibilities, more comic than tragic. But the ride was over; he vowed never to ask her anywhere again, even to lunch.

Doctor Stern was not a suitable substitute; he was just that, a substitute. They lunched at the

CARA MIA

Tuller Bar, a one-flight walkdown around the corner from the Fine Arts Building whose near-absence of natural or artificial lighting made it seem the ideal haunt for patrons seeking anonymity. Neither he nor Stern filled that bill; they only felt that way at times. The generous quarter-pound hamburgers were just what the Doc prescribed for such conditions of the mind and soul.

From the moment they sat down at the Tuller, Stern resumed his active recruitment of Kinchen on behalf of his brother-in-law, the ad man. The fit was perfect right down to location. Frankel's office was only blocks away in the David Stott Building. Deighton was bent on leaving downtown anyway, Stern insisted, so why not hitch your car to a train that's already arrived? Stu's billings were twice what *Deighton & Kinchen* were pulling down, all he had to do was check the red book on that. Kinchen promised he would when he returned to the office.

It was not until they were about to leave that the doctor brought up *her* name. The delay was all the

MICHAEL CORNELL

more amazing in the light of all the *Spanish* villas Kinchen had been rendering on the bar napkins. Stern said he was thinking of suggesting her to his brother-in-law for one of his advertisements, either for a car or a fur coat spread. He then embarked on one of his *if I were a little younger* tangents in a heavy-handed but good-natured way of encouraging his more youthful fellow tenant to act on the opportunity at hand. Kinchen said nothing.

Deighton still had not returned when he got back to the office. Cara was in the process of making the anteroom more presentable as Kinchen walked past without saying a word. He closed the door of his room and resumed his design of Spanish villas. Once he thought about sketching her from memory and then showing it to her, but he continued his loose architectural roughs instead. Around two-thirty, the Fyfe Shoe client called back to ask about his modified ad. Kinchen answered the phone before Cara could and immediately reassured the man that it was already on its way over to both pa-

CARA MIA

pers' make-ready departments. When he hung up the receiver, he cursed himself for forgetting and got to work on the changes at once. Then he burst from behind his closed door and out, hurrying down the fire stairs rather than wait for old Will and his older *Otis*. All the way over to the newspapers on foot, he wanted to blame Cara for distracting him from his appointed duties. The conviction, even in his own mind, did not stick and he was relieved just to deliver the revised ad keylines on time.

Caroline Deighton was holding court at the office upon his return. Caroline, whose glossy handsomeness made her look as though she could be her husband's sister, may have liked cozy corners in restaurants as Adam had said, but she nonetheless possessed the slick deportment local society columnists had admired enough to write about. On this occasion, she was dispatching verbal invitations to a little impromptu get-together she had decided to stage on Adam's and her behalf that evening.

MICHAEL CORNELL

"What shall we celebrate, Adam-dear?" she was inquiring in a tone of voice that almost seemed to have an incestuous intimacy to it.

"I don't know, what do you got?" When the response only elicited a disappointed grimace, he tried: "How about we celebrate my selling Robinson on his new media schedule."

"How mundane," Caroline deadpanned. "Well, what about it, David, you're the Creative Director around here. Come up with something creative for us to celebrate tonight."

"I do shoe ads, remember?" Kinchen didn't feel like being witty. "Adam and I are throwing this little shindig to commemorate the expansion of Deighton and Kinchen—from a staff of two to a payroll of three. That should be a big enough staff, I would think." As she spoke the words her eyes were riveted upon Cara. "You *will* bring D & K's newest find, won't you, David?"

The ride on the coaster was getting crazier, Kinchen thought. He vowed not to ask her any-

CARA MIA

where again but somebody was asking her for him. He felt like unhooking the restraining guard before the car touched down.

Wednesday Evening,
April 10, 1968

*Five hundred Colgate students
stage sit-in over discriminatory
housing practices*

FIVE

"Caroline thinks I hired Cara because I'm mad about her." Adam Deighton had Kinchen off in a corner of the oversized dining room. They both were looking beyond the melange of Donovan and Marianne Faithfull look-alikes to Caroline and Cara in the opposite corner. "Isn't that the most ridiculous thing you've ever heard?"

MICHAEL CORNELL

"No more ridiculous than that song on your stereo." Kinchen couldn't think of anything else to say.

"*I Am The Walrus*? You've got to be kidding, old pal?" Deighton seemed dead-serious. Maybe it was the wine. "You *do* know what it really means, don't you?"

His partner launched into some gibberish of which Kinchen absorbed little of nothing. He was still watching Cara, marveling how she seemed not in the least intimidated by her immediate surroundings, most especially in the silver-spoon nepotism set of high cheekbones, and chiseled noses. She had them all beat on both counts, but it was not the physical superiority that radiated from her. It was something more substantive than that unless he was wrong. He wasn't wrong at all.

"Tell me: would I hire somebody just because they looked like her?" Somehow Adam had switched tracks again, was running once more on the main line. "Be honest with me, old pal?"

CARA MIA

The "old pal" stuff smacked of Tom Buchanan in *Gatsby*, but with Deighton it fit. Soon he would be spouting his theories on the Aryan race.

"Tell me. I've got to know." He was begging now. Maybe his partner had had more wine than he thought, Kinchen surmised. Desperation was a debilitating side-effect.

"I don't know her," he felt obligated to respond.

"But you drove over here with her." Deighton *was* drunk. He had to be. Walruses made more sense than that and they made no sense at all.

"You know your wife better than I do, Adam," Kinchen tried to make light.

"I thought I did before tonight, old sport." It had finally happened: Adam Deighton had become Tom Buchanan. No one else used *old sport* anymore. "I thought I did but now I don't."

Kinchen wanted to excuse himself but empathy prevented him.

Deighton took another long swallow from his wine goblet, looked again across the room.

MICHAEL CORNELL

"Dammit, she's beautiful," he observed soberly. It was the first sober thing he had said.

Kinchen excused himself to refill his own glass, walked instead through the French doors and onto the empty terrace. The night was clear with Jupiter and the nearer stars in plain view in the Detroit sky. Someone was listening to the Tiger game on the radio on the other side of the tall wooden fence that skirted the back yard. He glanced over his shoulder at the huge old house whose restoration had become the Deightons' all-consuming passion next to throwing garden parties and impromptu wine socials. It, too, was out of *Gatsby* and he was glad to be out of it. As he looked back skyward, he felt a growing desperation of his own engulfing him. In its stifling grasp he longed to return to the relative peace and sanctuary of Beverly Morehouse's Rembrandt-lit apartment.

"At last, escape." Kinchen turned. It was Cara. Carmen against the glow of the house. "Does she subject all your new employees to this?"

CARA MIA

"You're the first person we've hired," he informed her. "Up to now Adam and I have done everything around there."

"She threw the party for me, you know." It sounded presumptuous. It also sounded right. "She didn't say that, of course. She didn't have to. I feel bad for Adam."

"Adam feels bad for Adam."

"He does not deserve it. Neither of us does. Please take me back to my car."

"You don't want to excuse yourself first?" The question was right out of the Chapter on Party Etiquette. He didn't know why he asked it.

"I don't want to walk through that house again. Can we go around the side of the house to leave?"

He nodded, led the way down the stone steps of the terrace. He would explain in the morning, he thought, or he wouldn't explain at all.

They drove back downtown in his Barracuda. He didn't know whether to feel like a getaway driver effecting a daring escape or a hack for hire with a beautiful fare who didn't want to talk. He

MICHAEL CORNELL

wasn't talking either. The ride was too short for all the things he was thinking, would have wanted to say. Her car was in the narrow parking lot adjacent to the Fine Arts Building, under the single light. A large, five-year-old Ford in fair shape except for the inevitable Midwestern rust. Hardly the type of automobile that Carmen would be driving. He watched it start too fast, drive away too quickly. He wanted to follow her, find out where she lived, where she stayed at night, but there were other fares out there to pick up.

He laughed at himself, drove away slowly in the opposite direction. The affecting fragrance of her perfume remained inside his care, inside his head. He never saw the beat-up black Malibu in his rear-view mirror, never heard the rumbling drone of its too-old muffler. Suddenly it sped beside him, veered in front of him at the blinking-red traffic light. He slammed hard on the Barracuda's brakes, barely avoiding a rear-end collision. The Malibu's driver-side door flew open, a black blur rushed over, yanked his own door open and him out of it. In a

CARA MIA

veritable instant, he was against the side of his car, staring into the fathomless black eyes of his assailant, with the cold, razor-edge of a knife across his throat.

"You keep your hands off her," came the hissing threat through clenched white teeth. At the same time, the young, even Hispanic features came into focus. And the minutest suggestion of fear. For Kinchen, it represented his only chance. If he were wrong, he was dead as fast as his blood would flow. He didn't move. He didn't dare.

He felt the blade withdraw, next the young punk himself. As quickly as he had appeared, he left. Kinchen never even bothered to watch him speed off, never even took down his plate number. He was too numb.

Beverly Morehouse looked more beautiful than Cara. More beautiful than Carmen. She wasn't. She only looked it now in his profound relief.

"David, what are you doing here?" She was wearing what looked like expensive Oriental pajamas of pastel-yellow silk.

MICHAEL CORNELL

"I ran out of wine," he said without smiling.

"It's ten-thirty."

"I tried to run out earlier."

She smiled for the two of them, kissed him. "Come in. I'll get you a refill."

He made his way to the living room, through the darkness toward the black shapes of the large pillows on the floor where she must have been sitting when he rang up. He sat but it was too late. The sound of breaking vinyl was unmistakable.

Beverly was standing in the living-room archway laughing, the wind bottle in her hand. "You just killed Sgt. Pepper," she announced.

Thursday,
April 11, 1968

*U.S. Secretary of Defense
sets ceiling of 550,000
American troops for Vietnam*

SIX

The next morning Kinchen said nothing about the incident to either Deighton or Cara, following the same course he had taken with Beverly on the night before. He had in fact, said little of anything to Beverly Morehouse. Securing refuge at her place, and to a similar extent sitting on *Sgt. Pepper*, had relieved the tension enough to induce a drowsiness that saw him doze off on her carpet before he finished the first glass of wine. Instinctively, she had been understanding enough to stir him to consciousness around midnight without pumping him for explanation *or* apology.

Correspondingly, Deighton sought no explanation for his or Cara's early departure from his wife's party, but Kinchen credited that more to blackout than to understanding. In either case, his partner arrived around ten in high spirits, disappeared behind his door to put in a telephone call and reappeared in even higher spirits. The would-be convention bureau client Summershoe wanted to revisit the agency's creative materials from the abortive pitch of several months before, as he had said at the Chop House, and he wanted to see the stuff today at three. Deighton had volunteered to provide an updated media schedule as well, which he specified would be Cara's responsibility to both compile and present. But first he wanted her to withdraw one hundred dollars from petty cash to purchase a chic business suit to wear at the presentation. Kinchen

CARA MIA

liked the violet-print mini-dress she had on, but said nothing, even when the petty cash coffer came up thirteen dollars short of the C-mark and he had to cough up the balance from his own billfold.

While Deighton rehashed the typewritten proposal, Kinchen headed downstairs to their basement storage locker where he had filed the materials. Rather than wait for the ancient Otis, he used the fire exit. As he had guessed, the open elevator was parked in the darkened basement. Old Will Evers was parked next to it in his maintenance cage. He was slumped before a large color poster of Martin Luther King. Kinchen had seen them hawking the posters on Woodward two days after the assassination.

"Will, are you sick?" he inquired with concern.

"Yes, sir, I am, but not in that way," he answered. "I've just been doing some thinkin' and it seems every time I do that I get sick." He looked up at the picture of King. "It's terrible what they done to him. But the thing is: it's not over yet."

Kinchen wanted to ask what the old man meant. He didn't have to:

MICHAEL CORNELL

"It's just starting," Evers continued, "only this time it's going to go faster. When they shot John Kennedy, we had to wait four and a half years. We ain't gonna have to wait that long this time—and I don't just mean another terrible shooting, or even what's goin' on in Vietnam. No, *this* time, it's gonna touch us all a lot closer to home. So if you ask me if I'm feelin' sick, then I guess the answer is yes, only it's the kind of sick they ain't got no cure for."

Will Evers' words were depressing, all the more so because once again he was powerless to respond. There was no way to console the old man when he had the same dark foreboding himself. He slipped away silently, guiltily to the storage locker, gathered up the layouts and hurried back up the fire stairs.

From waitress to media maven. Kinchen was impressed. They all were. He watched Cal Summershoe watch Cara as she took his contingent of four through the agency's media recommendations. Summershoe, a slim silver-haired man of forty-five right out of *GQ*, may not have been listening to a single demographic statistic but he was buying it all. Kinchen, on the other hand, was listening to every word and marveling at the cool modulation of Cara's delivery. It spoke of training he knew she never had. The elocution itself, even with the slight Spanish accent, was a perfect complement for her composed manner. From the outset of her part in the pitch, she had seemed less nervous than he had felt during his portion, even with all the outstanding creative work he had to present. As for Deighton, he had supplied his customary "grace before meals," in addition, of course, to playing the role of the impeccably attired, handsome young ad exec. *Central Casting* could not have booked a better actor for the part.

The presentation ended with Summershoe complimenting Cara on the stylish cut of her dark-red business suit. Unless Kinchen was mistaken, it looked to be pure silk and a stone steal at one hundred dollars. On her, he mused, his thirteen-buck cash contribution had just turned the Daily Double.

Almost as an afterthought, Summershoe promised to get back to the agency by the following week with his final decision. Despite his non-committal stance, Kinchen felt ready to place another out-of-pocket bet on the outcome, while his partner was prepared to engrave the name of the *Convention Bureau* on D & K's client list. It made an ideal excuse to do a little premature celebrating, something Deighton was never inclined to procrastinate about.

It didn't figure. Adam Deighton was a *toucher*. He couldn't just make a point by saying it; he had to make contact with your person, generally on the shoulder or upper arm. With the opposite gender, an arm around the waist was his standard mode of physical communication. For the past hour, in the comforting warm light of the Caucus Club, he had been reciting the praises of *his* discovery, Cara Linda Cansino, and had yet to lay one finger on her silk suit or anywhere else. The omission did not seem to disturb Cara, Kinchen thought, but it must have bothered Deighton a lot. Just watching his

CARA MIA

partner talk without touching was starting to bother *him*. It was almost as though Deighton was refraining from contact or so as to not give *him* the wrong impression or, worse, any impression at all.

"Maybe I was good today because I didn't know any better," his partner had finally let Cara say something on her own behalf. "Maybe if I knew even a little more than I do, I would have come across as what I am: a beginner. But if you say I was good today, I will accept it happily."

"Cara, the first thing you've got to learn," Deighton said, leaning forward without even brushing against her, "is that advertising is no place of business for humility. If you've got it, you flaunt it like Cassius Clay—I mean Muhammad Ali—does. Cara, take my word on it: you've got it." He added: "naturally, you'll first have to accept the premise that the word of an advertising reprobate such as myself means something."

Adam Deighton was now doing his poor man's Cary Grant. Tom Buchanan was no more in his range, Kinchen said to himself with no particular animosity for his partner. He decided to let Cara take in the show on her own while he used the restroom.

When he emerged, he was too far away for the two of them to see that he had seen. It is unlikely they would have noticed him if he had been less distant. The embrace was one of the most passionate he could remember seeing in a public place and he didn't want to remember *this* one so he left without returning to the booth.

Friday,
April 12, 1968

*West Berlin police hold
2,000 rioting students at bay
after leader's shooting*

SEVEN

Kinchen looked into his bathroom mirror and hardly recognized the person before him. The face was drawn, the eyes tired and the mouth set with a somber rigidity that was completely foreign to him. Too, the dark hair had started to curl unkemptly toward shoulder length. More and more he was looking like a strange cross breed of the kind of hippie protester one would see in Kennedy Square and the species of homeless derelict that frequented Grand Circus Park.

Work, he determined, had everything to do with the metamorphosis. The agency's clients had become more demanding, the deadlines more unreasonable than ever before, and the unsettling spectre of an entanglement between Deighton and Cara loomed larger than he could endure mentally or emotionally. When there are only three people in the office and two of them are engaged romantically, he concluded, then the third party is the piece of the jigsaw that belongs with another set.

Doc Stern furnished the only solution possible. It was the one he had been selling for days called Stuart Frankel. Just talk to the man, he urged again on the elevator up that morning, what do you have to lose? *Nothing* seemed the only logical answer. Kinchen used it and Stern said he would set up a lunch for him with his brother-in-law the ad man this afternoon if Stu was free. Kinchen wished it were sooner because, for the first time, *he* wanted to be free. Of D & K, of Adam Deighton and of Cara Linda Cansino.

This time, his partner *did* ask him where he had disappeared to the evening before and why. Kinchen only bothered to answer the second part by saying that he had not been feeling well. Deighton didn't believe him and he wasn't sure if he cared anymore. The ambiguity of his feeling toward her, even after last night, made him want to get on the phone and confirm Frankel's availability for himself. Instead, he decided to leave it to Doc Stern while he holed himself up behind the closed door of his small studio and doodled interlocking hexagons until his pending-assignment ethic became too formidable to ignore.

Stuart Frankel was not as he had pictured him from his newspaper pictures. A handsome man with intense blue-gray eyes who looked to be ten years younger than his fifty years, did not at all convey the *What Makes Stuart Run* persona the local media had painted of him, at least at this initial meeting at

MICHAEL CORNELL

Trader Horns. On the contrary, he seemed disturbingly normal for the ad business.

"I need a partner," Frankel came to the point early-on between sips of his ice-water. It was the only thing he was drinking. "We could sit out the first dance, the first two even, and finally hit the floor for the first slow one they play but why? Kinchen, you're aware of the kind of work I do; I'm well acquainted with the kind of creative work you do. As my medical deviate brother-in-law keeps telling me, the fit is a good one."

Kinchen was flattered, feeling better already. Stu Frankel was as good as they come in this town, likely as good as anyone in New York or Chicago as well. He had just acknowledged the merit of Kinchen's own creativity by coming right out and saying it. What's more, he had asked him to sign on with him. Suddenly, D & K was looking like a mere line on a resume, a piece of background from the years 1966-68. Adam Deighton, on the other hand, was looking like a once-good friend and business associate with whom he had shared a transient dream. As with all dreams, it had to end, to be replaced by newer ones, as appropriate for their time and place as their predecessors had been for theirs.

As for Cara, she would become a beautiful young woman who had worked briefly in the same office for the tiniest portion of the D & K years on his bio sheet. There would be no mention of her on the page.

"What's memorable?" Frankel was asking now over his deviled-crab appetizer. "Memorable to me is a Rembrandt self-portrait with its magical darkness and light. From a completely divergent angle, memorable is Sandy Koufax pitching a no-hitter in *four* consecutive seasons. Or it's the haunting theme from *Laura*, the old black-and-white classic from the Forties with Gene Tierney."

The subject matter was mesmerizing in its way. Kinchen wondered where the man was taking it.

"I'm looking for a girl," he lowered his voice, as though to take off the melodramatic edge, "a girl who will embody the allure of Detroit by night."

MICHAEL CORNELL

Kinchen thought he knew already, but he asked anyway: "What's the account?"

Frankel was open enough to tell him: "It's a client I don't have—yet. A client you guys pitched yourselves: the Convention Bureau. We both lost that one on politics. But politics doesn't create good advertising. I think Summershoe knows that now."

Kinchen wasn't as open to admit that they had re-pitched the business only the day before. He saw no reason to. In retrospect, he saw no cause for the little celebration at the Caucus Club either. Deighton and Cara, of course, would have their own reasons.

"I want this campaign to be as memorable as any that's ever been done for this city," Frankel resumed. "I want to shift the stage lights from the Motor City as fire-belching behemoth to one of the sultry seductress who's as mysterious as the night itself. Naturally, the whole approach to selling Detroit's nightlife to potential conventioneers will be couched in subtler terms than the ones I've been waxing here. That's why the girl must be perfect,

CARA MIA

as memorable as Gene Tierney was Laura, even more so."

He added after another sip of ice water: "I'll tell you something funny, funny-ironic. The Doctor thinks you've got the girl I'm looking for right in your office."

To Kinchen, it was more ironic than funny. He took a taste of his wine, said he would like to order.

Lunch was as pleasant as Frankel had been. It should have been easy to sign on with the man, to shake hands and start the paperwork. It should have been but the best he could say was he still needed a little time to think the matter over. Frankel seemed a little surprised. Nearly as surprised as he was himself. Nearly.

Friday,
April 19, 1968

*U.S. planes unleash
massive bombing raid
on North Vietnam*

EIGHT

Adam Deighton closed the door of Kinchen's office, stepped over to the drawing board.

"What gives, old pal?" Deighton was attempting to use his six-foot-three height to intimidating advantage by not sitting down. "You take the Herner's *Bottled Magic* tv storyboard to the client by yourself. What happened to the team concept around here?"

"You tell me, Adam." Kinchen wasn't intimidated.

"What the hell is that supposed to mean?" Deighton averted his stare. "Didn't all three of us go to see Summershoe together on the convention stuff?"

"That's right—me and you and Cara." As soon as he said it, he regretted the petulance of his tone.

"Hey, if you're trying to imply that there's something going on between me and Cara besides work—" Deighton stopped short of finishing, his eyes everywhere around the room except on Kinchen.

I'm not *implying* anything, he thought without saying it. Instead he said: "Beverly Morehouse called me directly and asked to see the board before we show it to Herner, which she wants us to do next week."

"Beverly likes you, doesn't she, old sport?" Now his partner was trying the diversion trick.

CARA MIA

"One could do a lot worse than Beverly Morehouse, that's for sure. As the Brits would say: she's a real *smasher*."

Kinchen wasn't biting. He was being quiet until Deighton took the confrontation back to where it belonged.

"Listen, David, I want you to believe me when I say there's nothing going on between me and Cara. If there were, Caroline would kill me."

One had nothing to do with the other, Kinchen surmised. It was the first time, too, that the similarity in the names had occurred to him: *Caroline* and *Cara Linda*. That, of course, had nothing to do with either.

"What do I have to do to prove to you you're wrong?" His partner was running his long fingers across the edge of the drawing board as he invariably did when he was agitated.

"Why don't we just forget it." It was predictable recourse, but suitable for the wounded-colleague routine he was witnessing. Somehow he had to come up with a way to spare himself the discomfort of catching the entire act. He came up with it easily enough: "By the way, I wouldn't bet the farm on us copping the convention business. If anyone takes it away, I don't think it'll be us."

The play worked. Deighton was looking at him again. "Who's it promised to? And where did you get your information?"

"I don't think it's officially promised to anybody—especially us."

"But Summershoe seemed to like what we showed…" his partner's voice trailed off as though he saw the retort coming.

"The suit did look nice on her, didn't it?"

"What's this?" He had the thing wrapped in an oversized box that would not tip her off. Beverly tore the gift wrap, lifted the lid. "You finally bought one."

"But only to replace the last one who was a casualty of war," he stated.

She started to remove the shrink-wrapping on the *Sgt. Pepper* album. "Shall I play it?" she suggested capriciously.

CARA MIA

"You do and I'll have to buy another one."

"Then it wasn't an accident?"

"What do you think?" he smiled. Suddenly he felt good, at least all right. It was Friday night, D & K was behind him and Beverly Morehouse was in front of him in the fetching lime mini she had worn for the afternoon meeting. He had felt like touching it then, touching her, but protocol had prevented him. One of these days, he promised himself, he would look up the word. Tonight, he took hold of Beverly, felt the smoothness of the dress, the smoothness of her arms, kissed her.

"What shall we do tonight?" she asked.

"There's a new Sidney Poitier movie at the Grand Circus," he told her.

"That's too long in a darkened theatre for me," she shook her head. The ends of her straight blond hair glittered like copper on the shoulders of her green dress. "Besides, I've got something to tell you. I almost told you after the meeting today."

He didn't like the sound of it so he didn't ask.

"I've put in my notice. I'm going to give New York a shot."

MICHAEL CORNELL

He had been afraid of that. Now that she had said it, it had sounded even worse than he imagined.

"I'll be at your presentation next week with Herner's. In fact, I told them I would stay until my replacement is on board." She seemed genuinely sadded to inform him of her decision. It provided little solace. "I suppose you'll want your album back now," she tried to cheer him. It wasn't working for either of them.

As with his confrontation with Deighton, there was something incongruous about the entire scene. Like a bad French movie with *French* subtitles. He had hardly known Beverly Morehouse, she had hardly known him. Still, he remembered, he had rushed to her when his throat had been almost slit. And he was here now.

The incongruity lasted for the balance of the evening. Conversation seesawed from meaningful to meaningless with inexplicable frequency. Foreplay stayed foreplay when feelings augured more. If they had been lovers, Kinchen thought, this would have been one final, desperate union; if they had been more than friends, this would have been one final, desperate chance with nothing to lose.

Through it, he kept thinking back to his lunch meeting with Stuart Frankel, to the reverential tone he had imparted upon his campaign idea about the night. The blackening skyline with its random squares of light outside Beverly Morehouse's high windows spoke eloquently of the merit of Frankel's concept.

Night in the city. It was what compelled Kinchen to drive in the direction of the Fine Arts Building when he left her around midnight. It was also what almost impelled him to drive past when he saw the lights, the crowd, the police cars.

Saturday,
April 20, 1968

Detroit: *Investigation opens
into murder of ad executive*

NINE

Will Evers was the first person he recognized, Caroline Deighton the second. Both were crying uncontrollably. Past the pass of uniformed police and plain-clothesmen, there was a large inert form under a sheet and, underneath that, a saucer-sized pool of shiny-red substance on the parking lot asphalt. No one had to tell Kinchen what the substance was or who it belonged to.

"I just knew it, I just knew it," old Evers was sobbing. "I sensed it when they called me at my house, even before that—you know I did, Mr. Kinchen."

He looked over at Caroline Deighton. She seemed to have the tear-letting under control for the time being as a wiry, black-haired detective in an unbuttoned raincoat asked her questions. He was Italian or Spanish, Kinchen guessed, with dark features and sharp, compelling eyes set in an olive face.

"A young couple coming back from a movie show found him, Mr. Kinchen," Evers said before burying his face in his hands.

A pair of white-coats had the body on a stretcher now, still covered, and were being escorted through the crowd of onlookers by a group of blue-uniforms. Caroline Deighton followed them to the waiting emergency unit by curbside. It was too late for emergencies, he observed bitterly, then went over to the wiry one and identified himself. The de-

CARA MIA

tective did the same: Inspector John Fuentes, Detroit Homicide. He had some questions he wanted to ask: Kinchen had one of his own: How? A slash across the throat. Ear to ear. When he was found at around ten forty-five he had been dead a half-hour, probably less. The autopsy would confirm it.

Ten forty-five. That would put the time of death between ten-fifteen and ten-thirty, he calculated. About the time he had started thinking about Stuart Frankel's *Night*. The mysterious seductress, he had called it, or words to that effect.

Fuentes continued: According to Caroline Deighton, her husband had called home around five-thirty to tell her he was going to stay over to straighten and rearrange the office for an important client meeting Monday morning, so his weekend would be free. What time had Kinchen left? Around twenty after five, came his reply. What didn't figure—and he told the detective so—was that they seldom invited clients to the office because of the small space and they *never* made important client presentations there. Why don't we go upstairs and

MICHAEL CORNELL

you can tell me if the office looks the same as it did when you left, Fuentes suggested, or if indeed it had been straightened and rearranged. Kinchen agreed.

The reception desk, Cara's, may have been more directly in front of the door as you entered; his partner's desk may have been a little closer to the front window, it was hard to tell. Files and such were generally neater, but it was difficult to say whether that had been the work of the cleaning lady or the result of some late-night tidying by Deighton. Had your associate said anything to you about staying over? No, he had not.

"Did you have any quarrel or disagreement with your partner before you left?"

At first it did not occur to Kinchen why Fuentes was asking. He answered: "A minor disagreement."

"About what?"

"About work."

"Where did you go this evening?"

The thrust of his questioning went home. "I visited a friend," he said, sounding less certain than he was.

CARA MIA

"Your friend will be able to corroborate this?"

"Certainly." The tone was better. Not adamant, but sure.

"We'll have to have the name of the party you were with."

With reluctance, he gave it to the inspector. Moreover, he divulged details about his own terrifying experience of several nights ago; he only asked that Fuentes not mention it to Cara. After admonishing him for not reporting the incident when it happened—you might have saved your friend's life, the detective reprimanded him with justifiable disgust—he consented to respect his request as long as it did not impede the investigation. Cara Cansino was on the way over, Fuentes then informed him.

The inspector concluded that he wanted him to accompany an officer named Farrell to the downtown station to look through some head-shots. Couldn't it wait until tomorrow morning, Kinchen wanted to know. No, it could not, Fuentes upbraided him.

On the way down with Farrell, he was relieved Cara had yet to arrive. He had started to cry. When

MICHAEL CORNELL

old Evers slid open the elevator grate on the main floor, he fully expected Adam Deighton to be standing there waiting to go up. Good morning, *old sport*, he would greet him in his familiar glad-hand tone.

Good evening and good-bye, old sport.

Monday-Wednesday,
April 22-24, 1968

*Columbia U. students seize
buildings; Sen. Robert Kennedy
challenges U.S. role in Vietnam*

TEN

By Monday, police were still seeking to question the man Kinchen picked out of the file shots: Luis Ramon Cansino, Cara's brother. Whether Fuentes had revealed his sources or not, she did not show up for work. He didn't expect her to be coming back, something which caused him as much regret as relief. He thought about going through the papers on Deighton's desk to see if he could locate her phone number, but he was unsure whether Fuentes' boys had finished their search of his late partner's things. There were more than enough cardboard file boxes with code-labels on them he couldn't decipher—he suspected that none of the inspector's underlings could either—so he closed Adam's door and left it closed.

Cal Summershoe turned out to be the client, albeit prospective type, who had scheduled a meeting with his partner for Monday morning. Deighton must have called him after Kinchen dropped the notion their convention re-pitch would likely go the same way as their original presentation: nowhere. Summershoe phoned around ten to say he had seen the television and newspaper stories and wanted to express his sincerest condolences—Kinchen wondered how many levels there were—and would set up another meeting to discuss the bureau business after the funeral.

After fielding similar calls from other clients, secured types, and one from Stu Frankel, he locked up the office to head over to the funeral home. On the way out, he asked the still grief-stricken old elevator operator, Will Evers, if he had seen Doc Stern. He had not.

The funeral home was a long-established Grosse Pointe parlor that had in its day displayed some of the area's wealthiest and most prominent after *their* day. True to the place's reputation, they had done a remarkable job on Adam Prescott Deighton's handsome features, the high-collar concealing the nasty nature of his fatal wound. Kinchen, disbelieving after three days, alternately wanted to embrace his silent friend or report to him that Summershoe had rescheduled their meeting. He finally settled on a prayer but one didn't come to mind, so he rose and walked past members of the immediate family seated nearby in a row of cushioned folding chairs. If he couldn't think of what to say in a prayer, he resolved, he couldn't think of what to say to them.

Caroline Deighton stopped him in the vestibule. She wore a dark blue business suit, not black, and an expression that could best be described as enigmatic.

"Haven't you something to tell me?" she asked in a voice that was not hushed.

"Caroline, I'm very sorry." He had already said it Saturday at the house. Maybe she hadn't remembered in her day-after shock.

He looked at her in bewilderment.

"Was Cara Cansino with Adam on Friday night?"

He could not answer right away. When he finally did, it had a less-than-honest ring to it. "I don't know. I left the office earlier than I usually do."

She turned and walked away. He didn't bother to sign the *guest* book, left the funeral home. The perfectly modulated ambience was oppressive.

Adam Deighton's funeral on Wednesday at cavernous Memorial Church on the Lake was well attended, well covered by all media. The eulogy was given by an alleged old fraternity brother of the deceased. He could have been talking about anybody, Kinchen thought; he wasn't talking about his partner and close friend, at least from where he was sitting several rows back from family and in-laws. By his side was Beverly Morehouse who had been very supportive all through the ordeal. He also saw Cal Summershoe, Doc Stern and Stu Frankel, among others, at the service.

Still, he kept thinking he should be driving downtown afterward to meet his partner for a couple of rounds at the Chop House or, better yet, the Tuller. It was too dark in there for anyone to ask you stupid questions they already knew the answers to.

cara linda

Monday,
May 6, 1968

*Heavy fighting rages
in Saigon and other
South Vietnamese cities*

ELEVEN

The next time Kinchen saw Cara she was the visual inspiration in diamonds and black sequin for a full-page ad in the Midwestern edition of the *Wall Street Journal* that read: *Motor City Nights. There's nothing like them anywhere.* The text was no more original than the headline in its less-than-rational appeal to conventioneers to bring their business to

Detroit, but the ad's overall effect was dramatic and impactful. For lending her striking face and equally striking figure, Cara had received modeling credit in the lower right corner as *Cara Linda* in addition to whatever fee had been paid her. For *his* efforts, Stu Frankel had won Cal Summershoe's coveted account. And Summershoe had bought himself an opportunity to see Cara Cansino—Cara Linda—at least one more time. Kinchen was reasonably certain that the studio photography session must have run long; Frankel would have seen to that.

As he studied the ad on his drawing board, he looked up to see Doc Stern for the first time since the funeral, the only time last week.

"Well, what do you think?" Stern inquired anxiously.

"I think your brother-in-law works fast," was the first thing he thought of.

"He contacted her the day after you two had lunch."

"Here?"

CARA MIA

"I believe so. Why?" The doctor seemed to be getting another kind of anxious.

"Ever hear of conflict of interest, Doc?"

"Conflict?" He was starting to squirm a little, not enough. "You guys didn't have the convention account."

"We showed for the primaries."

"Then you should have said something to Stu at lunch."

"Maybe I thought he wasn't serious," Kinchen lied. "Did Adam know?"

It was obvious Stern didn't know, so he dropped it, closed the paper.

"Well, since you're so happy with me," the doctor started up again with quiet trepidation, "you'll be delighted to hear I'm leaving."

Kinchen was at a loss to respond to the man.

"I know what I've been telling you all along—about staying downtown," Stern stumbled on, "but after what happened, you can hardly expect me to stay. Besides, it wouldn't be fair to my patients, especially the older ones."

MICHAEL CORNELL

Kinchen was staring out the window now. The skyline looked pretty much the same.

"Anyway, if you wondered where I was last week, I was looking in the northern suburbs. I found a nice suite in Huntingdon Woods that was vacated by a doctor who retired two months ago. There are some other nice offices around there—in case you're interested."

"Thanks, but I think I'll heed your original advice for now," he finally said.

"At the time I gave it to you, I meant it," Stern insisted, "but it's like old Will keeps saying: everything's changing and not for the better." On the way out, he stopped, rubbed his gray head. "I just hope you don't let the ghosts get to you," he cautioned solicitously.

Kinchen went back to skyline-gazing, heard the outer door close, then reopen. Momentarily, Inspector Fuentes was standing where Stern had stood.

"I'm not going to tell you I just happened to be in the area," he opened with a wry smile that somehow seemed to have as much friendliness to it.

CARA MIA

"Adam might have known that Cara was doing the convention bureau ad," Kinchen informed him by way of a greeting.

"What ad?"

"The Wall Street Journal ad."

"My subscription expired."

He couldn't tell if the detective was being sarcastic or not, handed him the paper opened to the page.

Fuentes stared at the ad a long time, read the body copy, lifted his dark eyes back up to Cara's picture. "Is that what they pay you to do all day: sit around drawing and look at glamor shots of beautiful women?"

Kinchen had not imagined the friendliness. It continued:

"I feel like Mexican food. Can you break away for lunch at Mexican Villa?"

The invitation stunned him, not the thought, but the words: nearly identical in his recollection to Adam Deighton's of some weeks before, weeks that seemed like years, years he desperately wanted back.

MICHAEL CORNELL

"Sure," he said. Drawing ginger ale bottles and looking at glamor shots of beautiful shoes would have to wait.

The table at which he and Deighton had sat was open; Kinchen made sure he and Fuentes sat elsewhere. To his relief, too, there were no waitresses who even remotely resembled Cara Linda Cansino.

"I vaguely remember seeing her here a long time ago," the detective told him in the most conversational tone, "but the Villa has never been one of my favorite haunts. The food here is more Tex-Mex, extra hot. Real Mexican cuisine is closer to Indian cuisine, milder. My penchant has always been for that type—and blondes with blue eyes."

You would love Beverly Morehouse then, he thought; he said: "But then Cara *was* with Deighton at the office that night?"

"She admits to it, but claims she left him around nine." The tone continued to be unofficial, but to Kinchen the information was anything but. "And yes, I suspect that your friend Adam *was* aware of the convention ad she was going to be posing for. I'll ask her when I see her again for additional questioning."

Kinchen didn't have to ask when that would be. "When her brother shows, I'll have her back," Fuentes apprised him.

The casualness of his disclosures was beginning to bother him; the inspector read that as well: "He'll show, don't worry," he assured him, the same casualness making Kinchen feel better already.

Tuesday,
May 7, 1968

*Sen. Robert Kennedy wins
Indiana primary over
Sen. Eugene McCarthy*

TWELVE

Kinchen saw the ad among Vernon Herner's papers on the client side of the large conference table. At first it troubled him; then, as Beverly Morehouse supplied the preamble for her own boss that Adam Deighton would have delivered, the presence of the ad made him more curious than vexed. Why would Herner have Frankel's work, Cara's ad, at the presentation of his *Bottled Magic* tv concept? As Beverly finished, he made a determined effort to reserve his curiosity until he had taken the client panel by panel through the storyboard.

Herner, diminutive fourth-generation marking director for the family-owned ginger ale company, had expressed his sympathy over the death of his partner before the meeting began. The pressure was off. Herner, he knew, would want to like what he had to show. Sympathies aside, the television commercial would sell itself. It would only be a matter of booking a production house to shoot the spot.

And cast the part. Of course. Beverly had presold the concept, told Herner about the sinuous, sensuous genie who, through the magic of special effects, emerges from the bottle of ginger ale. That was precisely why the ad from the Journal was there: Herner had just the model to book. They don't get any more sensuous than her, he would insist. And Kinchen would listen dutifully, if he were smart. He lifted the vellum cover, presented his work.

Herner was ecstatic over the storyboard, pulled the ad from his papers, laid it across the table. "This is the *Bottled Magic* girl," he declared emphatically.

Beverly said nothing, looked over at Kinchen.

"I'll have to make sure Stu Frankel doesn't have an exclusive on her," he put in an illogical bid to disturb the predictability of the moment.

"That's nonsense," Herner laughed. "This is ginger ale; that's convention gargle."

It *was* nonsense and, dutiful or not, he didn't feel very smart. *Cara Linda was the Bottled Magic girl.* Herner knew it. And Kinchen was finding out.

The client had done an excellent sell job.

When he returned to the lobby of the Fine Arts Building, the elevator light board showed the car and Will Evers in the basement. He never pushed the button, took the stairs instead. Cara had started the Monday following King's shooting which had been the fourth, he recalled on the way up, so

MICHAEL CORNELL

Deighton might have scribbled her telephone number on his calendar page for the eighth. Except for Fuentes, the police had not returned; what they had wanted from his partner's office, they had already taken, Kinchen deduced. The office, and even the stuff packed in their labeled file boxes was open game.

Catching his breath, he was about to insert the key when he heard rustling inside. He turned the knob; the door was no longer locked. He stepped in, made his way slowly to the source of the noise: Deighton's office. He half-expected to see Cara's brother, half somebody he had never seen before—

Caroline Deighton looked up. In her long right hand, she held a matboard cutting knife with the large razor facing out. She had been slashing open the police file boxes herself and on Adam's desk, set aside among other things, was the malachite desk-calendar holder. It was empty.

"I'm taking what belonged to Adam," she informed him directly. "Fuentes and the rest of them can go screw themselves."

CARA MIA

Kinchen picked up the calendar holder.

"If you're looking for the pages from that thing, check the police station," she said. "If you're looking for her phone number, check the phone book. I looked it up myself. The little slut lives in a dive on Grand Boulevard."

Suddenly, he felt the compulsion to defend his fallen partner. "You're wrong about Adam," he asserted before she could say anything more. "There was nothing between him and Cara." It was a bad line from a bad soap opera.

"Either you're very naive, David, or you think I'm some stupid, unsuspecting dolt. Tell me which."

"Adam *was* straightening the office that night for a client meeting Monday morning."

"That's what he told me when he called—and that's what I told Fuentes when he asked. But you and I know no clients came here. Adam wouldn't let them; the digs didn't look prosperous, he would say."

But Cal Summershoe *was* coming here; he called Monday morning and told me."

MICHAEL CORNELL

"That's even funnier," she laughed derisively, "with that full-pager Stuart Frankel did for him running in the Journal. Maybe Summershoe—and Cara—played us all for saps."

"You're not being rational," he shot back, "Summershoe had just met Cara."

"Tell me about rational. My husband had just met her, too. Frankel probably hadn't even met her yet and the next thing he's doing is plastering her face and everything else over a full-page ad. Whores like that work fast; they're too street-wise to play slow parlor games."

Caroline Deighton finished packing her husband's things and left.

The address on West Grand Boulevard hadn't always been a *dive*. Called *The Barbara*, the vestiges of its long-past elegance were still apparent in the marble facade. The evidence of its deterioration was clearly visible in the brick sidewalls with the open windows and tattered shades. Somewhere in those decaying three stories with their fifty-watt

CARA MIA

light bulbs and peeling ceilings, Cara Linda lived or at least checked in from time to time. When the notion became harder to bear than to believe, he drove away, vowing not to be back.

Tuesday,
May 14, 1968

*U.S.- North Vietnam peace
talks resume in Paris;
Nixon wins Nebraska primary*

THIRTEEN

In appearance and talent, Deborah Luckow and Lori Mazzili were virtual twins. Both dark-haired and slight, each was an accomplished still photographer in the advertising field. Deborah, who grew up and learned the trade in New York City, had a strong portfolio of fashion and people samples, while Lori had made her specialty tabletop shooting, the photographic embellishment of jewelry,

MICHAEL CORNELL

food and the like. Each had a savvy sense for the business side of their profession and, more importantly for Kinchen, each had made the often-times difficult transition from still work to film shooting. Their company, *Northern Lights Productions* was the ideal house to take the *Bottled Magic* tv script and storyboard to completion.

There had been another consideration: As women, he could be assured that there would be no exploitation of either the concept *or* the model-actress, Cara Linda Cansino. Their policy, in cases of *extra-sensual* commercials, as Deborah would call them, was a shooting set closed to all but the agency producer. Invariably, that meant no assistant or junior-type producers *and* no clients. It was a policy that would have ruffled more political feathers had their work ever fallen short of superb, which it never seemed to do.

The *Bottled Magic* spot was an extra-sensual commercial and, despite their attendant uneasiness, Kinchen was glad to serve as agency producer. Not only would he be able to oversee the exacting adherence to his script and visuals, but he would also be given the chance to see Cara as *Cara Linda* for the first time and at a safe, if voyeuristic, distance. Even his suggestions and reservations (if he had any) would go through an intermediary, Deborah Luckow, the commercial's cinematographer and director.

It intrigued him to be at Northern Lights under the circumstances and so soon after the nightmare. He vividly recalled recommending the production company for an expensive "image" commercial for Fyfe Shoes, a tv spot that would undo the kind of price-item announcements that paid bills but where a professional liability to the agency's reputation. He and Deighton had even started poring through model composites to cast the right girl for the fashion statement Fyfe would be making. Of course, neither of them had envisioned their most pragmatic of clients to take the plunge and spend the money, so the idea of approaching Deborah and Lori in the interest of "artistic greatness", as Adam had put it, was put on hold. Now, barely a month after they had clinked beers on the pipe-dream, he was here for another client, another purpose. In deference to his partner, he mentioned to Deborah that he would resurrect the Fyfe concept and present it to the client himself, something Adam never had a chance to do.

Lori's meticulous recreation of the first three storyboard panels in which the Herner's Ginger Ale bottle miraculously uncaps itself, rises through the mist and finally alights on the studio-simulated beach, amazed even Kinchen. When Lori had originally informed him that she was going to achieve the effect via strings and not special effects, he had been skeptical. Now, with the atmospheric lighting and the wisps of dry-ice fog, he was unable to detect even a hint of the strings. Instead, it had him thinking about the kind of mysterious music—perhaps a sitar right out of *Sgt. Pepper*, he winced—that would best complement the visual imagery he was beholding.

By the time the opening product portion had been completed, he had yet to see the *Bottled Magic* girl. He was uncertain whether Deborah and Lori

CARA MIA

had orchestrated her entrance until the last possible moment as part of the show-biz shtick that made for good shop-talk at parties, or if their model had arrived while he had been mesmerized by Lori's own version of bottled magic. If it had been the first reason, he hoped that the two women had not read some additional significance to the casting of Cara Cansino beyond what he himself had told them; he certainly did not want either of them thinking that the girl held some inexplicable power over him because of the horrible thing that had happened in the parking lot of the Fine Arts Building. He had even asserted that she had been the client's choice, not necessarily his, but it was dubious whether they believed him, with his own reputation for not rolling over at the first sign of client whim. It had always been his contention that advertising agencies existed as much to protect their clientele from self-inflicted evils as to provide them with viable concepts. In this instance, Vernon Herner had suggested the girl from the convention ad; he had sanctioned her as the right choice. It was important to him that Deborah and Lori accept that assertion as truth and conduct their business with him accordingly. Despite his trust in both, he could not afford any speculation, inadvertent or otherwise, that his personal life was an impediment to his commercial art.

When he saw her, it was for the first time since the late afternoon of the night Adam Deighton died. What he saw, however, was not Cara Linda Cansino. It was an apparition from the shadowy reaches of his own imagination, the very essence of his creative preconception for the genie from the ginger ale bottle. It was also the embodiment of the calibre of commercial genius he had unearthed in Deborah Luckow and Lori Mazzili. The diaphanous black body-suit with its not-so-random sprinkling of magical glitter, the most skillfully applied of theatrical make-up, the just-right tousle of ravishing black hair and the most sensuously choreographed of sound-stage movement all contributed to the transcendence of his brainstorm to a league far distant of his wildest expectations.

CARA MIA

There was something more. More than the brilliant germ of his own brilliant idea. More than the Merlin-like magic of Deborah's and Lori's artistry. From his vantage point in the darkest corner of the studio, he sensed he was witnessing the appalling crystallization of his very first illusion about her, the one that had made it so hard to look at her, to communicate with her as he would with any beautiful woman. He thought he had dealt with it when he had found out more about her, about her upbringing, her background. He thought he had. Now he realized that the mystery, the breath-stealing paralysis at the very sight of her, had surfaced anew, more frightening than ever. Surely it defied logic. So did ghosts—*don't let the ghosts get to you*, Doc Stern had warned—but to some they existed as literally as the living. And who was he, even after watching take after take, to deny the rationality, the saneness of what he was seeing so lucidly? If Deborah and Lori did not see it, it could only be because they were too preoccupied shooting a ginger ale commercial. The main thing was that *he* saw it.

MICHAEL CORNELL

And most certainly, Adam Deighton had seen it.

Monday,
May 27, 1968

*Sen. Robert Kennedy backs
gun-control in Oregon primary*

FOURTEEN

He had seen the commercial a hundred times. Now, on Beverly Morehouse's vintage-color Philco, he was seeing it for the first time, as hundreds of thousands of viewers would see it. The time slot, the local affiliates "window" before *Mod Squad*, was a good one. He was just too tense, he found, to sit back; infinitely more nervous than the ginger ale company's assistant marketing director sitting next to him. Both had been drinking something stronger than ginger ale, but as the precise second approached, she had taken to sipping her expensive French champagne while he dared not touch his.

"There is an uncharted land that bridges fantasy and reality," intoned the voiceover in a Serling-like cadence, "where the wondrous senses of sight, sound and taste become magically one…"

He watched the cap lift off, the mist grow mistier, the genie emerge, dreamily, provocatively, as though from the bottle itself. *His* images, *his* words. He could not remember being more intoxicated from a creative high of his own reaching. Yet when it was over, when the thirty seconds had run their too-swift course, he could take credit for nothing.

"God, she's beautiful," were Beverly's first words. The next were as damning: "She's too beautiful for a tv spot about ginger ale."

Hurt, he fully expected her to follow with a token acknowledgement of his contribution to the commercial, for ginger ale or not. She didn't, or

CARA MIA

couldn't; her telephone started ringing at once.

The first of the calls was from her boss, Vernon Herner. He couldn't have been happier, Kinchen could tell from her few short responses. And why shouldn't he be celebrating? Hadn't he cast Cara Linda on the spot himself?

The other calls were the same. Associates, friends, family raved about the commercial, *especially* the girl who comes out of the bottle. Where did you get her, they all wanted to know. Even the women.

When his token praise finally came, it was too late to be of consolation; it was too late for him to even feel resentment for the oversight. Yes, he now realized, he *had* created the concept, but she had made it work. What she was, what she brought to the commercial, he could take no responsibility for. To be sure, he knew, some form of personal recognition would come, perhaps at the next advertising awards competition, but it could never obscure the reality of the matter. Resigned, he dialed the number of Northern Lights Productions.

MICHAEL CORNELL

As he guessed, Deborah and Lori were both working late and had watched the spot. He thanked each for her own contribution, accepted their reciprocal compliments, then returned to his champagne and Beverly.

"You should be happy," she insisted. "Your commercial is a great success. Here's a real-live client telling you what a wonderful tv spot you did."

How could she have known what had been coursing violently through his mind? He said quietly: "What makes you think I'm not happy?"

"Would you have been happier watching it with—" she paused, "with Adam?"

He could not answer her.

"Or is it something else?" she asked next.

He *could* answer that one. He chose not to, so she answered for him:

"It's Cara Linda, isn't it?" it was a statement in the form of a question that didn't have to be asked. "It's funny," she now remarked, "how things work, the turns they take, the people they take with them. The two of you, Adam and you, meet a girl in a

CARA MIA

restaurant; the next thing you know, she's working for you, the three of you are working together. Then one night—" Abruptly she stopped, perhaps the morbidity of it all finally silencing her, he couldn't be sure.

"Then you take me," she resumed again in an airier tone that was fooling neither of them. "See that string of colored yarn," she pointed to a dozen-or-so short lengths of red, yellow, blue and green yarn strung vertically in tapestry fashion across the tall window framing Detroit's night skyline. "When that runs out, Beverly Morehouse runs out."

He wanted to kiss her. He wanted to cry. He wanted to be walking down some darkened corridor in some seedy apartment building on West Grand Boulevard.

He would knock on the old peeling-red door, the sound of the knock echoing emptily in the deserted hallway.

The door would open and she would be standing there. *Cara Linda*. Dressed as she had been in

MICHAEL CORNELL

Frankel's convention ad. For night. Black, dangerous night.

Silently she would invite him in, signal with her crystal champagne glass for him to take a seat in a room that looked to be in another building, to go with another door, a room as elegantly furnished as Beverly Morehouse's apartment had been.

He would sit in a velvet-cushioned chair, under an antique Tiffany lamp, and be immediately drawn to the room's incongruity, a run-down console television from the early Fifties. On its twelve-inch screen, in grainy black and white, a beautiful girl was issuing forth from, of all things, a bottle of ginger ale.

Tuesday,
May 28, 1968

Late Dr. Martin Luther King's Poor People's March-ers *turned back by police*

FIFTEEN

The elevator light on the lobby board of the Fine Arts Building was stuck on Five, his floor. After fifteen seconds, he abandoned his wait, mounted the stairs. When he emerged from the Fire Exit door, he heard the shuffling of boxes, saw old Will Evers pushing a hand-truck with some sealed cartons into the open elevator car. Doc Stern followed right behind with a carton of books clutched between his sleeveless arms. He didn't feel like talking to the man but it didn't matter.

"Kinchen, don't be sore, okay?" Stern extended an apologetic greeting. "I would've stayed, you know that."

"Forget it," was the most civil response he could muster.

Evers tried to help. "Doctor Stern, sir, I've got to be getting this stuff downstairs. Some people are waiting for the car." Kinchen wondered how the elderly black man could be staying so old-school cordial, wondered if Evers were wondering the same thing.

"Just leave the stuff in the lobby, Will. The van will be coming along in a few minutes." Stern watched the elevator door close, turned to Kinchen as he unlocked the door, not fast enough to prevent dialogue between the two. "Listen, Kinchen, I don't know why I'm trying to make you understand. Nobody around here needs to be lugging anymore guilt around."

CARA MIA

"But you're *not* going to be around here anymore, Doc, you're leaving," he reminded him with more caustic irony than the occasion required.

"Kinchen, you can go to hell," Stern suddenly emitted but with a softness of tone that belied the words.

He stepped inside his office, closed the door. In one long second he heard the knock, reopened the door.

"You know I didn't mean that," the doctor simply said. "I've always enjoyed talking to you, having you for a fellow tenant."

Kinchen stared at the man for what seemed like a long time but wasn't, then managed: "Forget it, Doc. You've got to do what you've got to do." It sounded trite, got triter: "As you say, you've got your patients to worry about."

"Patients, hell," the man confessed. I'm getting out because I'm a chicken. I'm flat-out running to save my white hide. I wouldn't tell old Will that, but it's true."

"You don't have to tell old Will," he said, the wryness gone. "I wish you the best of luck, Doc."

MICHAEL CORNELL

He reclosed the door slowly before Stern could think of anything else to say or wanted to.

At the front window of his studio-office, he looked down on the park. The same pretty blonde who passed through Grand Circus every morning, this time in a multi-colored mini that Peter Max might have designed if Mary Quant hadn't, crossed through again. The one-arm veteran who looked roughly Kinchen's age couldn't have cared less, slept through her crossing on his reserved grassy slope. The only missing one was the old, white-haired woman in the khaki jacket. The pigeons were looking desperately for her.

The front door knocked again. He didn't answer it, but it opened anyway. Momentarily, Doc Stern wasn't standing in his doorway; his brother-in-law Stu Frankel was.

"You really did it now, hot-shot," he shook his head.

Kinchen had no idea where he was coming from and even less a notion about where he was going.

CARA MIA

"I saw your tv spot last night," Frankel went on. "Impressive as hell. The only thing is, you just put the kibosh on my nightlife campaign for Summershoe."

Kinchen straightened angrily, but the man saw it coming, cut him off:

"Hold up there, my friend," he raised both hands, "the good doctor told me you were a little put out about me using her for the ad, but you've got to remember: when I hired her to model she was just a secretary."

"Yeah. *Our* secretary. Deighton's and mine." The anger was there, more heightened than before; only the tone seemed more reasoning and composed: "What did you think she would say when you asked her to be your featured model in a whole-page ad in the Wall Street Journal: 'Let me think about it and talk to my agent.' Is that how you thought she would respond to your overture?"

Frankel did not wait to reply: "I expected her to accept and she did. The fact remains: she was a secretary; I made her a model."

MICHAEL CORNELL

Kinchen picked up a small Exacto knife, started rolling it in his hands for something to do to control the futility of his feelings.

"But you can rest easy now," the man carried on, "because I'm selling Summershoe off her now that she's the *Bottle Magic* girl for Herner's Ginger Ale. *Motor City Nights* will have to make-do without her. The billboard that's going up on I-75 will be the last of Cara Linda for this ad man. I'm leaving the field to you, Kinchen."

Then, in a non-sequitur that would have made his brother proud, he finished: "By the way, my offer to you, to join forces, still goes. Think about it, talk to your agent."

Kinchen rolled the small knife around one more time, watched Frankel leave.

Doc Stern was right, he observed. *Nobody around here needs to be lugging anymore guilt around.*

Wednesday,
May 29, 1968

*Israeli Foreign Minister Eban
urges Arab states to
sign peace accord*

SIXTEEN

It was as though Doc Stern never existed. All the years the man had spent here and the only remnant of his stay was the yellowing eye chart on the wall. Kinchen tried to read the bottom line, settled for the one above it. The best he could do was tell they were all *E's*. The hollow sound of footsteps in an empty room interrupted the silence. The steps were too fast for Will, and the doctor had been gone for hours.

MICHAEL CORNELL

Inspector Fuentes walked in from the reception room, leaned against the doorsill. "Too large for my purposes," he smirked with a quick glance around the vacant office. "But if you've got something a little smaller."

Kinchen thought he was kidding; he wasn't.

"Dave, I'm thinking of chucking the police routine, becoming an ad man so I can sit around looking at pictures of beautiful women all day." Well, he was only half-kidding. "What's a small office in this place run, anyway?"

Kinchen shrugged, his curiosity piqued. "You'll have to talk to Will Evers about that," he said. "He can give you the number of the management company that runs the place."

"You're not even going to ask me what's my line?"

"I am if you don't tell me quick."

"What do you think?" Fuentes flashed his white smile. "Do I have the stuff of Marlowe or Spade or am I dreaming? The trenchcoat and hat I can get, but the question is: Can I pay my rent?"

CARA MIA

"Clients pay the rent," Kinchen related.

"Then I'll be relegated to finding missing persons and tailing unfaithful husbands of faithless wives."

"I thought you wanted to be Philip Marlowe."

"I do, but in real life the police handle the big ones the paperback gumshoes get." Abruptly, Fuentes became serious. "Speaking of which, I have nothing new to report on Miss Cansino's brother except that we got his picture out nationally. Hopefully, he won't take as long to find as Richard Kimble's taken Inspector Gerard."

Kinchen appreciated the update, even the cynical attempt at humor. It was coming at a good time, with Doc Stern leaving and even Beverly Morehouse unavailable for an after-work drink with other plans. He asked: "Do you have time for a couple at the Teller?"

"If I had time for one, I'd have time for a couple," Fuentes grimaced. "Sorry, they've got me working tonight. See, that's the thing about working for yourself: you set your own hours. You only

MICHAEL CORNELL

work the nights you want to work; the rest of the nights you're free to get into your own kind of trouble—whatever your preference. Mine's blondes, but I've told you that already."

Kinchen smiled, nodded.

"But after last night, you've got me thinking," the detective mused.

"Last night?"

"Yeah. If you don't accuse me of staying in to catch the *Mod Squad*, I'll admit to seeing your ginger ale commercial with you-know-who. It could make a spic start liking his own kind—except I'm more Castilian and so is she." He laughed, added: "Of course, I wouldn't make any kind of play until the book's closed and her brother's in the slammer. By that time, she'll be madly in love with me, don't you think?"

Kinchen wanted to stop thinking, get so drunk his brain would go blank, except there was nobody left tonight to go drinking with—except Will Evers. Tomorrow morning, he fully expected, old Will himself would be notifying him that he, too, would be leaving the Fine Arts Building and taking his elevator with him.

All that would be left was the empty shaft. It was just a thought.

"Make my job easier, will you?" he heard Fuentes say behind him when he thought the detective had already left. "No plays for Miss Cansino yourself until this thing blows over. It's mucky enough."

Not to worry, he thought, not to worry.

Wednesday Evening,
May 29, 1968

*Sen. Robert Kennedy calls
upcoming Calif. primary crucial*

SEVENTEEN

He had a couple at the Tuller, and a couple of Fuentes' as well. The place was dark and lonesome when you were with someone; when you were by yourself, it was like a solitary confinement except you paid admission. Drinking alone at night had never been a *preference*, as the detective had called it, but after the first two Scotches it seemed like a

MICHAEL CORNELL

tv commercial about a genie who comes out of a ginger ale bottle. All the same, he almost ordered another but he couldn't think of anything to toast. Deighton was dead. Stern was gone. And Beverly was on her way out. It was a wonderful life all around, so he left.

In the cool May air outside, the long day had wound into late twilight. He had walked a few blocks before it occurred to him that he was heading in the direction of his apartment. On foot, it would take another two hours. He turned and headed back toward the Fine Arts Building's parking lot. It was a pleasant destination to be headed. You never know who you might meet there, he laughed sardonically. A grizzled drunk saw him laughing, wondered what he was laughing about. The man wasn't as drunk as *he* was so it was no use sharing the joke; it wouldn't have been nearly as funny for him.

A block from the Fine Arts, a one-arm man loomed ahead of him. It wasn't the man Richard Kimble was looking for in the television show, the one who had killed his wife; it was the fugitive from

CARA MIA

Vietnam, the drop-out his age from the park, who didn't care about pretty women in micro-minis or anything else anymore. As he passed him on the sidewalk, he wanted to turn and ask him what his secret was, or was he saving it for a self-help book he was writing? The man would have got it, but it wasn't very funny either, so he didn't ask.

In the parking lot, he looked over his shoulder. There were no other shadows, no other cars for anybody to hide behind. No limp bodies lying under white sheets on the asphalt pavement.

And nowhere to go.

The offices were quiet. The cleaning lady, working from the top, had already finished their floor. *His* floor. Deighton was dead, Stern was gone, he reminded himself. One and a half less offices for her to clean. He felt his way in the darkened hallway to 506, inserted two keys before getting the right one.

Inside, he didn't switch on the light, followed instead the glow of the night skyline emanating from his studio window. He banged his knee hard against the edge of the drawing board, hardly felt it at all, collapsed in his chair and dozed.

Adam Deighton was there, running his long index finger along the upper edge of the board, saying: "You've got it all wrong, old chum." He wanted to ask him what he was talking about, what he was doing there at that hour. Instead he listened as Adam started off in another direction, on something about staying downtown. "We're not going anywhere, old sport," he was saying now. He wanted to believe him, to get up and embrace him before he left, before he wouldn't come back again.

He wanted to but something touched him.

It was her. The girl from the bottle. The girl from the Night. Her radiant black hair was pulled back from her forehead except for one long curl that rested lazily over one eye. She was dressed in a tight, ultra-short dress so shiny it looked wet against her rich curves.

He rubbed his eyes, reached down to the credenza and jabbed his finger purposely against the razor-edge of the mat-knife. It bled.

CARA MIA

As he rose, she kissed his finger, then his mouth full, her lips parting.

Adam was dead.

Cara Linda was back.

cara mia

Thursday,
May 30, 1968

Dr. King's Poor People's Campaign-ers
storm Supreme Court building

EIGHTEEN

It had been Kinchen's most productive day in a month. Pressing deadlines for small clients were met while loose ends for larger ones were tied in place. There had even been time for a few calls to a smattering of each size to thank them for their sympathy cards and assure them things had returned to normal at *D & K*, to the extent that that was possible with only *K* carrying on. He knew that the legalities of dissolving the partnership under the unfortunate circumstances would also have to be worked out with Caroline Deighton. For now, he was more than willing to maintain the fifty-fifty split in earnings until the matter could be resolved. The business complexity of it was something he could happily postpone in order to immerse himself in the more appealing creative aspects of the work. Suddenly his job was gratifying again, as it had been in the early months of his association with Adam Deighton and the odd periods after, when both embrace the challenge of a new-business pitch or the stimulating marketing problem of an existing client.

Yesterday, he felt, he had scraped the depths. Today he had regained his powers, was on an ascendant course once again. The dramatic turnaround, he was well aware, could be traced to one simple equation of cause and effect. The effect was obvious; the cause was even more apparent. Her name was Cara. The whole baffling, mystical experience had colored everything, even the *Bottled Magic* tv commercial which he watched once more

CARA MIA

upon his arrival to the office in the early morning. Without question, she *had* looked beautiful in the spot, had even dominated it visually. But now he was ready to acknowledge again his own elements of contribution: the premise, the narrative, the astute choice of music—even the effective, if trendy, use of the sitar sound the local jingle house had simulated under his direction. Cara had been very good and so had he. Deborah and Lori had done the rest and well.

The highlight of the day, of course, had been indisputable: Cara's visit around noon. She wore a red-and-black blouse and pants ensemble that was as contemporary as anything Carnaby Street had on the racks, yet conveyed the most curious connotation of what Fuentes might have called *Castilian* Spain at its traditional best. The small gold-coin earrings furthered the Spanish cause. Her hair was combed straight back as the night before, with the jet-black lock dangling coyly over one eye. It was a new touch, or one she had resurrected since she had worked briefly for them, and one she had deployed to good effect for Frankel's *Motor City Nights* advertisement.

Under her arm was a large board or picture of some sort covered in dry-cleaners cellophane. Kinchen was more than a little anxious to know what it could be, but it was evident that he would only find out when she deemed the most opportune time had arrived. Cara had learned a lot about the art of presentational *tease* in a short amount of time and he knew he had only Adam and himself to blame.

"You look beautiful," he greeted her with a kiss. Unabashed directness, it occurred to him, was something he himself must have picked up from his late partner.

"It's what a woman always wants to hear," she smiled demurely, or as demurely as her irrefutable beauty would allow. "Why is it then that men are always so stingy with such praise?"

"Maybe it's because they have so little occasion to dole it out," he ventured. "But you're not about to tell me that you yourself have ever been starved for those kind of compliments."

CARA MIA

"No," she said reflectively, "but I've known far worse forms of starvation."

"So you mean while you lived in Mexico?" he wanted to know.

"Not only in Mexico," she replied with a candor that was as new to him as the wayward tress of black hair. He was relieved to see her stunning features lighten again. "But I didn't come here to talk about such depressing things as starvation."

"You came to show me what you have hidden under that wrapper," he theorized good-naturedly.

"You may think it's silly." The tease was on.

"I may think it's sillier than silly."

"Worse, you may think it's a little vain of me."

"It's you without a stitch of clothes on," he grinned, "when you were about six months old."

"I'm sorry to disappoint you but I'm a little older than that in this picture."

"I'm trying to suppress my grief, can't you tell."

"But see, you've already guessed it's a picture."

"If I get any smarter, I think I'll kill myself."

MICHAEL CORNELL

"Please do not say such things."

"Okay, I promise not to get any smarter."

She looked down at the board in her arms.

"You've seen me this way before."

"That's only making me more anxious."

She lifted the cellophane, turned the board over and laid it under his drawing lamp.

"It's you in your genie outfit," he stared in genuine amazement. "Who shot this for you?"

"Deborah shot some stills of me when I first tried on the costume. I hope you like it."

"Like it? I think we should take it to Vernon Herner and have him offer it as a poster."

"Really? I was hoping you would say that."

"I'll do a tissue overlay showing where the *Bottled Magic* theme goes and where his logo will be situated so it won't be too blatant."

"And will there even be a little caption with… " she trailed off.

"With *your* name?"

"Cara Linda?"

CARA MIA

"If you want." Her pride was understandable. Reaching into his billfold, he withdrew a twenty, handed it to her.

"What's this for?" she asked.

"To have this blow-up matted and framed for the presentation—which I'd like you to attend."

"Just like old times."

"Not so old times. Now, do you need any more money to tide you over?"

"Thank you, but I just received a check for my convention ad."

It was considerate of Stu Frankel to make remittance so fast, he thought. He wondered if he had notified her yet of his decision not to use her again for the campaign. Or if he himself had changed his mind. He saved the question, said instead: "Then at least let me buy you lunch."

"Can't—if I'm going to get my picture framed and see my Aunt, too."

Her declining his invitation momentarily derailed his spirits. Maybe it had also been mention of the aunt, the one she said had taken her brother

MICHAEL CORNELL

in when she returned to Mexico with her mother. Just as quickly, Cara made it right:

"I'll see you tonight, though."

He pulled her close. Already he was looking forward.

Thursday Evening,
May 30, 1968

*Richard Nixon claims Supreme Court
gives criminals "green light"*

NINETEEN

Deighton had scrambled the tickets, a pair of boxes behind the home dugout, before the season started and Kinchen was heartened to be using them. Cara seemed to have a better-than-average grasp of the game—her father had played some baseball in Mexico, she said—but the way she looked next to him made her knowledge of the sport's fundamentals a moot point. Underneath the red *Mexico City '68* Olympic Games pullover, he could see she wore no bra, to him an encouraging recent trend among young women who were so qualified. Cara's not overly large but ample breasts seemed to need no support but had his, unqualified.

The Tigers, who had been nosed out the preceding year by a late surge from Carl Yastrzemski and the Boston Red Sox, seemed destined to make 1968 their year from the campaign's first pitch. On this exceptional May evening for baseball, Denny McLain hurled an exceptional four-hitter for his ninth win of the young season. Nevertheless it was still premature, Kinchen felt, for talk of his becoming the majors' first thirty-game winner since Dizzy Dean posted that impressive number for the Cardinals in '34. Summer and the rigors of the real pennant race had yet to arrive; only, someone had to remind the local broadcast media—the major dailies were now striking—who felt McLain's early pursuit of the magic total made for more hopeful copy than predicting the precise day and time for

CARA MIA

Motown's next riot. On this night, with Cara reassuringly beside him, Kinchen was in absolute agreement.

Still, things preyed. When explanations for them were not forthcoming, he tried to furnish his own. She had insisted on meeting him after work, rather than have him pick her up; all right, he reasoned, she did not want him to see the old apartment building she called home. During the ballgame's most dramatic moment, with Al Kaline coming up to the plate with the bases full in the fifth, she leaned over and asked him if the next day's meeting with Herner over the matter of her poster were still on; okay, she was being anxious. Then, during the seventh inning stretch when he himself turned the topic from baseball and asked her how her aunt was doing, she informed him that she hadn't found the time, saying instead she had managed to sign on with two downtown modeling agencies after dropping off the poster for framing; at least, she had been honest.

Cara could be blamed only inadvertently for the last point of minor agitation. As they were leaving their seats, after the game's final out, Kinchen turned and saw Beverly Morehouse and several girlfriends leaving their seats one section up. He turned his glance away in order not to catch her eye, but he was certain that he and Cara must have been in plain view for the entire game in their choice boxes behind the Tiger dugout. The only consolation was that he had not known about Beverly's presence sooner for it would've only served to make him uneasy, and to be less demonstrative in his outward affections for Cara. All the same, it made him wonder who else might have seen them there together. It also made him change his mind about having *Cara Linda* at the poster pitch for Vernon Herner in the morning because Beverly Morehouse would be in attendance as well. Cara was not pleased with his decision and said as much on the ride back downtown.

"Tell me: is she a girlfriend of yours?" she inquired openly.

"She's a friend, and associate," came his candid rely.

CARA MIA

"Which is it: friend or associate?"

"Clients can be friends; it's happened on the rare occasion."

"And this is that rare occasion, is that right?" There was an air of flippancy about her pouting that both disturbed and fascinated. Jealousy was not its source.

"This is that rare occasion," he said.

"So you think this friend and associate of yours, and her boss, Vernon Herner, will not want to see the Bottled Magic sorceress in person tomorrow, is that it?"

Sorceress. Of course. That's so much better than genie, he thought; genies are something you dream about on tv. He smiled: "On the contrary, I think Vernon Herner would like very much to see you in person."

"So?"

"So let's make him wait."

She threw back her head. The sable lock landed in the same spot. "If you say so," she began again, mischievous intent in her tone, "but then I will want you to turn off here, onto I-75."

MICHAEL CORNELL

"But downtown's *this* way," he feigned mild protest.

"You have had your way; let me have mine."

He veered off. Three quarters of a mile north, his curiosity mounting, she abruptly ordered him onto the outside shoulder of the road. Feeling the fool, and playing the part well, he complied.

"Look!" she pointed excitedly. "It's going to be me!"

He raised his eyes, one hundred feet upward, to the large billboard. The outline of her face and form had been painted in black, much of the flesh-tone had already been filled in. It was the freeway version of Stu Frankel's *Motor City Nights* campaign.

"I wanted to wait to show you but I couldn't," she confessed, her exquisite face aglow. He had never seen her so excited, so exultant.

It was not the exultation, the elation, it was the fear, the frenzied desperation in her dark, beautiful eyes that terrified.

Friday,
May 31, 1968

*North Vietnam rejects
U.S. demands at
Paris peace talks*

TWENTY

There was much to do. Very little of it was creative. He had decided to make his visit to Herner an unscheduled one, a surprise *cameo appearance*, as Adam Deighton used to call them. Such calls generally caught the client off his or her guard and in a less resistant mood to buy something. At other times, when the client wasn't in or was unavailable,

MICHAEL CORNELL

it caught the agency account exec off *his* guard. The Fyfe Shoes "image" presentation, on the other hand, would have to be scheduled. What was at stake there was more than the selling of a pretty poster that would be an extension of a going campaign. What was at stake with Fyfe was more money. More money for the client to spend on an expensive tv commercial and accompanying print ads; more money for the agency to earn on creative execution and media placement. Nonetheless, Kinchen was thinking of at least setting up the pivotal presentation meeting by paying a spontaneous on Fyfe's marketing *priestess*, Whitney Von Dorn. Here was another of those instances of missing his partner's *savoir faire*. Whitney wasn't nearly as unapproachable as her name and manner would imply, but she was more deftly approached by one such as Adam Deighton who, in the mode of all good salesmen, could be many things to many different people—sometimes all at once.

The other bullet-point on the day's agenda, and perhaps the most bothersome, was the month's end

CARA MIA

bookkeeping, still another area in which his partner had excelled. Kinchen had always been the first to acknowledge that when it came to balancing the ledger, he couldn't hold a *creative* candle to his business colleague. The resolution of invoices, both incoming and outgoing, as well as the computation of day-to-day expenses for tax purposes were matters better and more expeditiously handled by Adam Deighton. Now, with his untimely death, as the media would say—was death ever timely, Kinchen wondered—the agency's creative guru was also the agency's account supervisor and, worse, the agency's comptroller. Wearing the ill-fitting third hat, he decided to make out an advance check to the name of Cara Linda Cansino for the modeling services rendered on the well-received *Bottled Magic* spot and to present it to her when he saw her after work.

"I've been told you used that little Mexican slut in a Herner's commercial." Caroline Deighton was being something she had never been, cutting in an ethnic way. "After what that little spic whore did, you have the insensitivity to use her in a D & K tv spot? She must be an awfully good screw, David; either that or Beverly Morehouse's leaving has got you imagining that she is." It didn't sound like Caroline Deighton, what she was saying and how she was saying it. He was at a loss to choose which issue to dignify first, if any.

"Beverly's leaving is a career decision of her own that has nothing to do with me," he started in rebuttal. "As far as the use of Cara Cansino goes, that was a *client* decision." He felt traitorous saying it as soon as it came out, truth or no truth.

"Since when did David Kinchen play the say for any client?" she raised her voice at the other end. "So at least have the courtesy of telling your ex-partner's widow, will you?"

"Telling her what?" he demanded.

"If the little Mex-whore is a good screw. Maybe it'll help me to understand everything, including why that Fuentes dick has been so slow in putting the pieces together about Adam's murder. It was

CARA MIA

naive of me to think that spies of a kind wouldn't stick together."

Kinchen looked up to see John Fuentes standing in his doorway. He didn't know how long he had been there, or if he could hear Caroline on the receiver. All he knew was that the detective wasn't smiling.

"I think our lawyers better sit down next week and resolve the matter of yours and Adam's partnership," she said when she got no response from the last part. "I'll have Watling call you," she finished, hung up.

"Well, David, you've done it to me now," Fuentes opened. Kinchen didn't say anything; it was his day, he thought with disgust, for *doing* people. "My man Farrell's sitting at the old ballpark last night with his three kids when he looks up and who should he see?" The guy paused for effect, but the effect was lost on him. "You and Cara Linda Cansino, that's who. I asked you not to muck me up, pal, and what do you do?"

MICHAEL CORNELL

First Caroline, now Fuentes. Kinchen turned, started scanning the park for the one-arm man, wondered if he were ready to divulge his secret.

Friday Evening,
May 31, 1968

Poor People's March-ers *take over*
auditorium of HEW Department

TWENTY-ONE

It was going to be extremely difficult not to invite Cara back to his apartment this night. The plunging, deep-red mini-dress with black hose had made his concentration at the Simon and Garfunkel concert in Cobo Arena nearly impossible. Even the enjoyment of such favorites of the duo's repertoire as *Homeward Bound*, *Scarborough Fair* and, naturally, *The Sounds of Silence* had been tested by the nearness of her. And while once more he was grateful to his deceased partner for having procured the free concert tickets well in advance, he was even more indebted to him for having met Cara. It was unlikely, Kinchen thought, that Caroline Deighton could ever have understood. Certainly, Adam had not been able to enlighten her.

As they settled into the corner booth of the cozy *Inn-Between* just blocks from the Fine Arts, there was news to be imparted, news that he had withheld until now.

"Vernon Herner informed me that your Bottled Magic commercial has received overwhelming response," he began. "Everyone wants to know who the *sorceress* from the bottle is. That's what I've got even Herner calling her now, so thanks for the word assistance."

The warm smile on her beautiful face made him want to rush onward. After a silent breath, he did: "And he wants twenty-thousand of your posters—twice what I went in there to sell him. He says he's going to give them away at concerts where his ginger ale is sold at the concessions."

CARA MIA

The smile on her well-shaped lips opened wider, revealing the whiteness of her almost-too-perfect teeth. Too perfect like everything else about her. He reached into his sport jacket pocket so he could look away to catch still another breath, took out the check. "For you," he said, handing it to her, "for being the inspiration—for everything." The last part sounded like something Cary Grant would say to Deborah Kerr; he didn't care.

She leaned closer, kissed him. Then she asked, almost too quickly: "Did you have a chance to see the woman at Fyfe about your image idea?"

He was sorry he had ever mentioned it to her, even sorrier now. Whitney Von Dorn had been intrigued by the concept when he had talked her through it during his brief afternoon visit. She had even referenced the "wonderful" ginger ale commercial he had done, only she said that she saw the *Fyfe girl* being vastly different from the sultry "soft drink genie", as she called her. In the most ironic of coincidences, one even O. Henry wouldn't have touched, Whitney related that she saw her shoe model as being someone like the young assistant marketing director at Herner's whom she had seen at various advertising functions. She had not referred to Beverly Morehouse by name, only as the prototype for the stylish, early-twenty-ish career woman who would embody the qualities she would be seeking for the Fyfe image campaign. Kinchen had not argued the point, had even concurred with her logic, something that flew right out the window now if the small lounge had one.

The reaction was petty, that of a high school girl: "Does this Beverly have my legs?"

Beverly has *her* legs, he wanted to come back with an appropriately adolescent rejoinder but didn't. "Whitney means someone like her," he spelled it out.

"You mean with her privileged upbringing?"

"I mean someone who will sell shoes for my client," he simplified things even further.

"I get it: I can sell ginger ale," she continued irrationally, "but I can't sell a pair of forty-dollar shoes to the spoiled Grosse Pointe types."

CARA MIA

Kinchen rolled his eyes in exasperation, looked back. She was reaching into her small red-beaded purse, pulling out a scrap of memo paper with a name and phone number on it. She handed it to him.

Reese Mather, a downtown phone exchange. Neither meant anything to him.

"He got hold of me through one of the modeling agencies I registered with yesterday," she stated, her expression now unreadable. "He saw the ad I did for Stuart Frankel in the Wall Street Journal. He's staying at the Pontchartrain."

"He's a photographer for *Playmate* magazine, on what he calls a scouting mission. He wants me to model for him, to be a feature in the magazine."

"A feature?" That's what she had said. "I don't want you to do it," he asserted emphatically.

"I thought you would say that, so I wasn't going to tell you about it." She took a sip of her Seven and Seven. "But now that you have told me that Fyfe Shoes doesn't want me—"

MICHAEL CORNELL

"That's *one* account," he cut her off. "What's the rush? You've only just registered with the agencies."

"When you have the pampered upbringing of a Beverly Morehouse, there is no rush…"

"Why do you keep bringing up her name?"

Cara ignored the inquiry, continued on: "…but when you've know the kind of deprivation I've known, every day is an eternity. Besides, Frankel has informed me that the billboard will have to be the last of my work for the convention campaign. He says the ginger ale spot overexposed me for his client."

"Cal Summershoe never expressed any such reservation," he contended, "I would bank on it."

"If he did or he didn't, it doesn't matter; the man is not going to use me again."

"Not for that campaign maybe—"

She cut *him* off now. "The future doesn't interest someone with my past and present," she declared straight-out.

TWENTY-TWO

Work was the only recourse, the office the only refuge. The color markers moved slowly, painstakingly across the drawing pad and nothing short of the most prodigious effort could induce them to render faster. The effort, the impetus, he determined, could not be marshalled from within him after Friday night. The requisite resources had been siphoned out of him and could not be restored readily. Storyboard frames of loosely sketched women's shoes and stylish early-twenty-ish career types stayed loosely sketched, unfinished and largely uncolored.

"Do I disturb genius?" was Beverly Morehouse's question upon entering. "Or is it incorruptible?" She wore the briefest of denim skirts, and a sky-blue tank top with nothing emblazoned across the front except the instant recognition that she wore no bra underneath. If the assault on the visceral sense was not impelling enough, she also smelled great. "If I did not know better, I might say that the species of *femina sapiens* you are drawing is closely related to my own. I recognize the business suit."

"It is supposed to be more than closely related," he attempted amiability.

"You mean it's *supposed* to be me?" Beverly seemed disarmed.

"If Whitney Von Dorn had her way, it *would* be you," he informed her.

CARA MIA

"Whitney Von Dorn? I never thought she noticed me at those interminable Adcraft luncheons." Now she was disappointed but the high priestess of Fyfe was not the reason. "I guess it was a bit much to expect that I would have been the inspiration for your own artistic leanings on this very pleasant Saturday afternoon."

Inspiration. *For you, for being the inspiration for everything.* Those had been his words to Cara.

"I would think you'd be deriving your motivation from other reservoirs these days," she resumed her banter.

"Beverly, you're not being funny," he remarked without looking up from the board.

"Good, because I see no reason to be." She dropped a tiny manila envelope onto his storyboard pad. He opened it, took out seven, eight short lengths of colored yarn attached to a string that he recalled seeing in the window of her apartment Monday night. "It's yours to keep," she said, "to remember me by."

MICHAEL CORNELL

Beverly hadn't been at his meeting on Friday, only Herner and this too-polite kid in an ill-fitting suit.

"My replacement is in place, as they say," she notified him without being asked. "You know I wouldn't have missed your meeting yesterday for anything, but I was in New York interviewing. *Crosse Liquors, Limited* says I won't need the rest of those colored ropes; they fired their marketing director on Tuesday and mine was the first resume to float down the transom. I start Monday."

A rush of melancholy passed through him as though, somehow, he knew that he should be sadder than he was.

"I'd ask to see you tonight," she let fall, "if I thought that was someone else I saw at the ballpark the other night."

"It wasn't," he said, "but dammit, ask me anyway."

The sadness persisted through the quiet dinner with Beverly that evening and the quiet hours they

CARA MIA

spent late Sunday afternoon before he drove her out to the airport where Dr. and Mrs. Morehouse were waiting to see her off. It was melancholy mixed with the unshakeable feeling of unfinished business over her that made him promise to visit Beverly soon in New York, and over someone else that made him point his car once more in the direction of downtown. It was the huge finished billboard high above I-75 of *Cara Linda*, in his mind only slightly larger than life, that compelled him to drive past the Pontchartrain Hotel. On the side street flanking its main entrance, her large, rusting Ford was parked.

Wednesday,
June 5, 1968

*Senator Robert Kennedy
critically wounded by gunman
after Calif. victory*

TWENTY-THREE

Outside *The Barbara* on West Grand Boulevard, there was a car that looked similar to hers. In the darkness under the burnt-out streetlamp it was hard to tell. He parked his Barracuda short distance away. A colored woman had got out of her beat-up Studebaker, was heading for the apartment building's front door. Kinchen hurried to arrive there at

MICHAEL CORNELL

the same time. She unlocked the lock, held the door open for him as he had hoped, then the inner door as well. He thanked her courteously, held the door, said he had to check his mail first. She bid him good-night, proceeded down the poorly lit hallway while he read the names and numbers on the brass mailboxes. C. Cansino was in the third row up: 314.

He ascended the stairway to the right of the first floor hall and the two flights after that. Stepping out on three, he walked nearly to the back of the building before locating her number. With surprisingly little hesitation, he knocked and waited. A television was on inside; there was scurried movement as well. Finally, the door opened a short way. A girl who looked Spanish, was pretty, stood before him. Pretty not beautiful. Not Cara.

"Yes?" was all she said. Beyond her, he could see a room furnished in the non-descript starkness of a cheap hotel. On the black-and-white tv screen, there was some kind of commotion going on, people rushing to and fro at one of the election primaries. The sound had been turned down.

CARA MIA

"I'm looking for Cara Cansino," he informed the girl.

"She doesn't live here anymore," she told him in a tone that sounded anxious, even fearful.

He was about to ask where Cara had moved when he caught the dark form of a man in the shadows of an archway leading to the other rooms. He was just standing there. The scant light being cast suggested little. Only a certain height. Even features. And someone who didn't want to be seen. Suddenly, he felt a draft in the musty hallway that hadn't been there, that probably wasn't there now. He returned the girl's apprehension, apologized for bothering her, left quickly.

On the stairwell down, he kept looking over his shoulder. Only the chill, the dankness followed.

At a phone booth a good mile away, he pulled his car over, called Police Headquarters, asked for Inspector Fuentes. As he waited, he could hear a television or a radio blaring. The same voice came back on, a Sergeant Locricchio, saying Fuentes had gone off duty, was there a message? In as coherent an account as his troubled mind and tight throat could manage, he related the message, urged that Fuentes be contacted at once, told where Luis Ramon Cansino could be found if they acted quickly.

All the while, Kinchen kept glancing outside the phone booth.

Cars passed.

Thursday,
June 6, 1968

*Americans grieve over
passing of Robert Kennedy*

TWENTY-FOUR

"Were you watching, Mr, Kinchen?" Will Evers' worn black face seemed to cast a whitish pallor. It was the face of a ghost of no certain color, its sadness so deep that it had become expressionless. "I don't know why God is allowing these things."

MICHAEL CORNELL

Kinchen felt as he had on that morning of two months ago: helpless and at an absolute loss to say anything that could possibly change what the old man was feeling. It was what he himself was feeling.

"Mr. Kennedy was so young—like his brother and Mr. King—with so much to be done," Evers commiserated anyway as he closed the elevator door.

Kinchen felt the sudden jerk of the car as it lifted on its cable. "Not just young, Will, but with the power, the wherewithal within them, to change things," he finally spoke. It hadn't been profound, even original, but he could see it was what Evers wanted to hear, and what he himself had to say after his silence of last time. Still, it changed nothing.

Will brought the car to a halt, let him out feeling as before. He made his way down the hall, unlocked the door, lingered lethargically before finally stepping inside. From the reception desk, Cara's work station for the briefest time, he called New York. Beverly was preparing to go into a meeting. She

CARA MIA

was doing all right so far. The entire city seemed to be in mourning. What she told him seemed to be the random answers to a random questionnaire sent out through the mail, but it was good hearing her voice. He let her go to her meeting, hung up.

Meetings, he thought. They were the same anywhere. Too frequent and too meaningless. An excuse for people to get together to hear themselves talk about themselves, to drink coffee, to schedule another meeting. He had one himself Friday. Tomorrow. He was to show Whitney Von Dorn the shoe storyboard, take her through its print-ad extensions. *Synergistic* he would call the campaign: one media perpetuating the other. Von Dorn would nod, bite the frame of her designer glasses which would be off by then.

Kinchen walked listlessly in his studio, fell into his swivel-chair, stared at the storyboard. It looked as before: sketchy, uncolored, unfinished. It looked like hell. He picked up a #6 Warm Gray marker, changed his mind and chose a #5, changed his mind again. The #7 Warm Gray was missing, but the #7 Cold Gray was there. It was almost dry.

The day disappeared in senseless strokes of his coloring pens, in the assembly of senseless ratings numbers for the next day's presentation—something Deighton, or Cara, would have compiled—and the dissemination of bogus assurances to senselessly worried lower-level clients calling to have their clammy hands held over the telephone wires, another Deighton specialty. Every time the phone rang, he expected it to be Fuentes getting back, acknowledging his tip of the night before. The hell with him, he cursed to himself.

Lunch and dinner were spent in the dark-tunnel anonymity of the Tuller Bar, a hamburger and two Stroh's predictably furnishing the sustenance each time. Each visit, too, had been followed by the aimless wandering of downtown streets, the daily recourse of the one-arm Viet-vet, he laughed out loud. The man's secret was almost in his grasp.

At the office, under the solitary light of his drawing lamp, the storyboard looked the same. He

CARA MIA

grabbed a marker, uncapped it, was about to slash an angry stroke across its face when the telephone rang.

It was Fuentes. "I thought you'd be there. Sorry for being slow getting back to you, but I wanted to have some information to tell you when I did."

Kinchen said nothing.

"I've got some. Our boy Luis Ramon wasn't at The Barbara when my men got there, only Cara's cousin Maria. The girl told us where she had moved, Royal Oak somewhere, but I guess you already know that."

"I haven't seen Cara since Friday night," he finally responded reluctantly.

Now Fuentes was silent. Kinchen thought he heard him let out a breath, a sigh of disgust. He was pretty certain. The detective spoke once again: "I hope to hell you're playing straight with me, Kinchen—because I've got something else to tell you."

Fuentes made him wait. He wanted to slam the phone down on him. Finally the man said: "Luis

MICHAEL CORNELL

Ramon was nowhere near here on April nineteen. He was being held on suspicion of stealing a car in Cincinnati from about eight-thirty to sometime after eleven. I just got the wire to confirm it."

Fuentes said nothing more, hung up.

"Cómo estás, David?" He still had the receiver in his hand when the stark silence of the office was pierced.

Cara was standing in his doorway. She wore a white silk blouse, a tight black mini. The lock of raven hair dangled over one dark eye. He could still see the pupil behind it. It looked different, like the other one, both strange, trance-like, still beautiful.

She held up a pair of keys. "I came to return my keys," she smiled with a coy innocence. Her arm seemed to sway. It might have been him, he thought.

He could hear her nyloned legs rustle against the inside of her skirt or slip as she came over, slowly, somewhat unsteadily, the sorceress from the bottle wending, weaving her way back into the patchwork tapestry of his jumbled brain.

CARA MIA

She kissed him, her wet tongue seeking out his, as his hands began wandering violently over her body, her secret places.

His hands stopped. He had not stopped them. He said: "Tell me about Adam."

She let out a low laugh. It had a wonderful, buoyant quality to it, as though she were reacting to a witty line of dialogue from a play. "But I already told you about Adam," she breathed.

"Tell me again."

"He didn't want me to do the *Nights* ad for Frankel. He said it was a conflict or something with your own stuff. We argued about it in the parking lot. He said he was going to call Frankel and nix it for me. He was going to kill my big chance, the one I waited my whole life for. He just wouldn't see my side of things." She could have been talking about a disputed call at third base at Tiger Stadium. She laughed her low, lilting laugh once more, said: "You should never have showed me how to use a mat-knife, David."

MICHAEL CORNELL

He pulled away from her warm, addictive body, but gently; there was nothing cold about it.

"You shouldn't have left the door open, Cara."

She became startled; they both did. Standing ten feet away was her brother Luis Ramon. He wore a shiny black jacket, a thin smile on lips shaped nearly as exquisitely as her own.

Cara calmed first. "It is good to see you, Luis," she greeted him, not unaffectionately.

"I have come a long way," he answered back. "We both have, I can see." Kinchen now remembered the voice.

"Too long a way to return to where we've been," was her reply.

"Not for brothers and sisters who were something more," he said in a quiet, almost reverent tone.

"We cannot go back to what we were, little brother."

"Oh, but I think we can." Somehow, he was standing next to her; Kinchen had not seen him move. "If you could have me take the fall for you—

CARA MIA

"But don't you see, *hermanito*, you have so much less of a fall than me to make," she interrupted him.

Kinchen could only watch. It was as though the pair were alone in his office with no one watching. He reached down to the credenza, groped for the small Exacto knife. It wasn't there.

"Oh, but *hermana-amante*, I would not think of leaving without you." Kinchen saw the boy raise his forearm, caught sight of something silver flash from the sleeve of his shiny jacket, never saw the vicious slice across the boy's throat, only the gushing of red across his drawing pad and board.

Luis Ramon was clutching Cara now, tottering, grasping her white silk blouse. Her white silk blouse covered with blood from him, from somewhere else.

They toppled heavily together against the tall front window, over the low front sill, the glass shattering into millions of razor-like shards.

He couldn't look down. In seconds it seemed, lights were converging on the Fine Arts Building, voices were drowning out voices, sirens were cutting out the voices.

Kinchen opened his hand. In it were eight short lengths of red, yellow, blue, green yarn. He counted them, counted them again.